Florida A&M University, Tallahassee
Florida Atlantic University, Boca Raton
Florida Gulf Coast University, Ft. Myers
Florida International University, Miami
Florida State University, Tallahassee
University of Central Florida, Orlando
University of Florida, Gainesville
University of North Florida, Jacksonville
University of South Florida, Tampa
University of West Florida, Pensacola

✕ Edited by Anne Blythe Meriwether

University Press of Florida

GAINESVILLE · TALLAHASSEE · TAMPA · BOCA RATON

PENSACOLA · ORLANDO · MIAMI · JACKSONVILLE · FT. MYERS

Marjorie Kinnan Rawlings

Blood of
My Blood

Copyright 2002 by the University of Florida Foundation
Published with permission of The Seajay Society, Inc.
Printed in the United States of America on acid-free paper

07 06 05 04 03 02   6 5 4 3 2 1

LIBRARY OF CONGRESS CATALOGING-IN-PUBLICATION DATA
Rawlings, Marjorie Kinnan, 1896-1953.
Blood of my blood / Marjorie Kinnan Rawlings; edited by Anne Blythe Meriwether.
p. cm.
ISBN 0-8130-2443-9 (c.: alk. paper)
1. Frontier and pioneer life—Fiction. 2. Mothers and daughters—Fiction.
3. Teenage girls—Fiction. 4. Michigan—Fiction. I. Meriwether, Anne Blythe.
PS3535.A845 B48 2002
813'.52—dc21   2001043732

The University Press of Florida is the scholarly publishing agency for the State
University System of Florida, comprising Florida A&M University, Florida Atlantic University, Florida Gulf Coast University, Florida International University, Florida State
University, University of Central Florida, University of Florida, University
of North Florida, University of South Florida, and University of West Florida.

University Press of Florida
15 Northwest 15th Street
Gainesville, FL 32611–2079
http://www.upf.com

CONTENTS

Editor's Foreword   vii

Note on the Text   xv

Acknowledgments   xvii

Prologue   xxi

Blood of My Blood   1

Fanny and Abram   4

Years of Plenty   9

Ida's Men   14

Mr. Kinnan   26

Marriage and Texas   33

Washington   40

Maternity   48

The Foundation   53

The Farm   67

The Talent   77

Beaus for Ida's Daughter   81

The Battle Begins   90

The Battle   111

The Battle: Men   136

Overture. Lights!   144

Interlude   155

Loneliness and Knowledge   161

In 1933, Marjorie Kinnan Rawlings published *South Moon Under*, launching a literary career that peaked with the Pulitzer Prize winner *The Yearling* (1938) and the widely acclaimed *Cross Creek* (1942).

But in early 1929 Rawlings submitted a 183-page typescript entitled *Blood of My Blood* to the competition for the Atlantic Prize, awarded to "the most interesting novel of any sort, kind, or description by a living author" and sponsored by the Atlantic Monthly Press.[1] The prize included $10,000 and all royalties from publication of the winning manuscript in book form in the United States and Britain. On May 14, 1929, the typescript was returned to her; packaged with it was a letter of polite rejection.

A decade and a half later Marjorie Rawlings scrawled a penciled note on the cover-title of the typescript: "Written 1928 and Jane Austen to a turn! MKR 1943."[2] Assuming the accuracy of this inscription, *Blood of My Blood* was written the year of her move, with Charles Rawlings, her first husband, to Cross Creek, Florida.

Blood of My Blood enjoyed only a brief life at its inception—written, submitted for publication, and rejected all within the space of a year. It was put aside then but carefully preserved along with that polite rejection slip. She apparently never offered the manuscript for publication again. She never told her second husband, Norton Baskin, about it, though he met her in 1933, only four years after its initial rejection. There has been no reference to the book in her published letters, nor in the several Rawlings bibliographies and biographies, which draw on her unpublished correspondence, nor in her several hundred unpublished letters that I have seen. At some point, however—presumably in 1943—the typescript passed out of her hands and into those of her young friend Julia Scribner. There is no evidence that Julia showed it to anyone, and it was not until 1988, long after Julia's death, that it again saw the light of day.

Although written in the form of a novel, *Blood of My Blood* is essentially nonfiction. Like the later *Cross Creek*, it uses many traditional fictional techniques and devices. It is part autobiography, part family chronicle, complete with the real names of dozens of family members (including the author herself), actual birth and death dates, and so on. Indeed, it may have been initially rejected by the publisher because of its obviously autobiographical nature.

A large portion of the book takes place before Marjorie Kinnan was born. After a brief first-person prologue by the author, *Blood of My Blood* is told by an omniscient third-person narrator, one who occasionally intrudes to reveal the unspoken thoughts of a character, or to supply information not revealed by the characters themselves. This narrator tells the story from the "present time"—that is, 1928. It begins as a tribute to Marjorie Rawlings's Michigan, pioneer-stock ancestors, whose love of the land and struggle over several generations of backbreaking labors transform their part of the wilderness into productive farmland. This early part of the book very much resembles her last book, the novel *The Sojourner*. And twice in *The Sojourner* occurs the phrase "blood of my blood," most movingly when Ase buries his daughter, Doll, "the child who was alone blood of his blood."[3]

The latter part of the book is a portrait of the young artist, Marjorie herself, very nearly ruined by her own egotism and by being alternately pushed and indulged by her mother. Other important family members appear too—especially her father and her mother's parents. But the most unforgettable portrait in the book is that of Marjorie's mother, Ida Traphagen Kinnan, a plain, thin-lipped woman who fights with a single-minded, indomitable will for the unrealistic goals she sets for herself and her daughter, more and more living Marjorie's life vicariously, un-consciously driving the girl toward either rebellion or destruction. And yet when at last Ida is confronted with defeat—her daughter's determi-nation to live her life by her own principles—she accepts the fact with courage and dignity.

The book focuses on the story of Marjorie's mother, and of their mother-daughter relationship. But in order to present Ida as fully as possible, *Blood of My Blood* also had to deal extensively with Ida's par-ents—her relationship with them, their relationship with each other. And it delves even further into the past to examine the family life of both of Ida's parents before they were married—encompassing too, Ida's husband, Arthur Kinnan, and his family background. *Blood of My Blood* is essentially a story about these related families and the relation-ships of the important family members, as understood by one of their youngest—Marjorie. It also represents her coming to terms, very suc-cessfully, in many ways even brilliantly, with the complexities of her inheritance and of her own nature.

Why was this book—the first of Rawlings's career—lost for so long? The answer to that question lies in another story, separate but related: the story of a successful older artist trying to help a promising younger one who was struggling with unchanneled creativity and energy.

Around Christmastime 1939, when Rawlings was in New York lectur-ing at Columbia University,[4] she was invited to spend a Sunday at the home of her publisher, Charles Scribner. She enjoyed a lovely visit with Mr. and Mrs. Scribner and their children, and felt an instant affection for and rapport with Julia, who was in her late teens at the time. There began a remarkable relationship between the teen-aged girl and the forty-four-year-old writer. When Julia, many years later, was asked by Marjorie to serve as her literary executrix, she accepted the responsibility. The friendship that had begun that Sunday afternoon back in 1939 would last throughout Rawlings's life. Julia faithfully fulfilled her duties as literary executrix until her death in 1961—a fitting and final demonstration of the love and trust the two women shared.[5]

Their first meeting that December was followed up with another one in February of the next year, when Marjorie invited Julia to stay at Cross Creek while the Scribners were visiting in Miami. The plan was for Julia to be dropped off on their way down, and picked up again on their return trip home. But when the time came for her to return to New York, Julia extended the visit at the Creek for another two weeks. The two women were having such a good time together, hunting, fishing, reading, and talking, that neither wanted the visit to end.

From that first visit onward, and throughout Marjorie's life, the two friends corresponded, visited, and sometimes traveled together. Marjorie, recognizing in Julia an intense and passionate nature that cried out for some kind of artistic fulfillment, took the young woman under her wing. During the early years of their friendship, especially between 1940 and 1943, one of Julia's keenest desires was to become a writer; and the letters from Marjorie to her young friend abound with words of advice. Rawlings constantly tried to encourage and steer her: "[Y]ou have a terrific mental and emotional energy that is not being used," she writes in July 1940, ". . . I think you should get into some work . . . [go] on with your voice, or [go] into editing at Scribner's. . . ."[6]

On January 14, 1943, Marjorie wrote Julia one of the most important and enlightening letters of their entire correspondence, showing the growth of the artistic relationship between mentor and protégée, and unlocking the major secret behind the composition of *Blood of My Blood*.

You will never be happy until you leave capitalism and its haunts behind you and strike out on your own. I would have urged, coerced, and bullied you into it long ago if it were not for those damn headaches that lay you so low. I am torn between thinking that they come from some mechanical pressure from the various physical accidents you have had, and thinking that they come from an emotional and frustrating pressure. I long so often to be a combination of God and a good doctor. But whatever the state of your health, happiness for you can come through only one of two channels— making your own living and doing some sort of work that you are equipped to do—or a happy marriage, for in marriage any woman who is not tormented by being definitely a creative worker, can find content and a sense of accomplishment. This is especially true if the man is doing something that the woman considers at least worthwhile. But you are too sensitive a person to be living the life you are living. *It is probable that in your case, as it was in mine, only your mother's death will liberate you, and that is a price one would wish not to pay for liberation* [italics added]. I hope and pray that you may find some compromise. Do make a supreme effort to stop the silly things you are doing and get into something that you like and understand and in which you can be useful. And don't feel that your training and qualifications are limited. Limitations are only a challenge. With your magnificent mind and sensitivity, you can find or make a place for yourself. How I wish you were my daughter! You are exactly what I should choose if I could have a daughter, and I would be the right sort of mother for one like you.[7]

It was presumably at about this time, perhaps a little later, that Marjorie gave or sent to Julia the *Blood of My Blood* typescript (along with several shorter, early writings),[8] knowing that the book reinforced what she had said in this letter, and that the letter illuminated perhaps the most important meaning conveyed by the book.

Early in her work on *The Sojourner*, Rawlings wrote to her editor at Scribner's, Maxwell Perkins, describing her research into her family history: "Aunt Ethel [Riggs] proved a fount of knowledge of the rich days on the farm . . . [including information] on my own grandfather, the prototype of the principal character in my book. . . ."[9] For what would become the last book she wrote, she was drawing upon and supplementing materials she had used in her first. Though for *The Sojourner* she changed names and expanded many episodes and descriptions, the similarities are often remarkable.

Abram in *Blood of My Blood*, her maternal grandfather, is the prototype for Ase in *The Sojourner*. The character of beautiful, lively, scrappy Fanny Traphagen, her maternal grandmother, comes to life again as Nellie in *The Sojourner*. (In a short magazine article entitled "Fanny, You Fool!" published in 1942, the grandmother is similar to those in *Blood of My Blood* and *The Sojourner*. There we see, for example, Fanny's familiar love of pranks and practical jokes and Abram's frustration with her—but his utter devotion as well.)[10] And the character of Squire MacHenry, the flute-playing, hard-drinking Irishman in *Blood of My Blood*, calls to mind the fiddler in *The Sojourner*, who gives the young boy Ase a flute.

While the struggles with Ida are in the foreground of *Blood of My Blood*, what resonates in the background is the girl's oneness with her father and grandfather. Rawlings used a striking image in her writings both early and late, combining moonlight, silver, and the blood of her forebears. When Abram was injured by a tree he was felling by moonlight, he "wondered why the moon had trickery in it and the sun did not. But the next night he was working again in the moonlight; for it was a part of him, like silver in his veins."[11]

An undated and unpublished Rawlings poem entitled "Grandsire"[12] reads in part: "He speared pike by lantern, he planted corn and wheat by night. / The moonlight was part of him, like silver in his veins."

In *Blood of My Blood*, the young Marjorie disappears one night, slipping out of her bedroom window. Her father finds her "dancing madly in her nightgown around and around the chestnut tree beyond, the full moonlight plain on the flesh of her gay and spindly legs. 'She's doing the only sensible thing on a moonlit night like this,'" he remarks to his wife. That night, he holds her close to his side, saying, "You'll never know how much your father loves you. You're mine—blood of my blood, bone of my bone, flesh of my flesh."[13]

Though *Blood of My Blood* centers upon Marjorie's relationship with her mother, her character is shown to be much closer to those of the menfolk of her family. It is from them, and especially her father, that she got the quicksilver in her veins that would give her the strength and independence she needed to win her freedom and write—and to tell the story of how this was done, in *Blood of My Blood*.

NOTES

1. *Publisher's Weekly,* February 16, 1929.

2. This typescript, with the letter of rejection, is in the archive of the Seajay Society, Columbia, S.C.

3. Marjorie Kinnan Rawlings, *The Sojourner* (New York: Charles Scribner's Sons, 1953), p. 180.

4. Elizabeth Silverthorne, *Marjorie Kinnan Rawlings: Sojourner at Cross Creek* (Woodstock, N.Y.: Overlook Press, 1988), p. 172ff.

5. Julia Scribner Bigham died on October 24, 1961, according to her *New York Times* obituary.

6. Rawlings to Scribner, July 24, 1940. Marjorie's letters to Julia are in the archive of the Seajay Society, Columbia, S.C. Permission to quote from them is granted by University of Florida Foundation, holder of the literary rights of the Rawlings Estate.

7. Ibid., January 14, 1943.

8. These short fictional typescripts are in the archive of the Seajay Society, Columbia, S.C.

9. Rawlings to Perkins, August 2, 1943, in Gordon E. Bigelow and Laura V. Monti, eds., *Selected Letters of Marjorie Kinnan Rawlings* (Gainesville: University Presses of Florida, 1983), p. 242.

10. *Vogue* 100 (July 15, 1942), p. 42.

11. *Blood of My Blood* typescript, p. 7.

12. This poem is in the Rawlings archive at the University of Florida Library.

13. *Blood of My Blood* typescript, pp. 60–61.

The typescript of *Blood of My Blood* was typed, obviously by the author, with a certain amount of care. Many corrections were made by strike-overs. It was then checked by the author, and many manuscript changes, additions, and corrections were made in her hand. Had it been accepted for publication and sent to a printer in 1929, Rawlings of course would have expected careful copyediting, especially for such matters as consistency in the use of italics, quotation marks, and the spelling of proper names as well as further correction of obvious punctuation and spelling errors. But because the author could not oversee this publication, copyediting has been sparingly done. Obvious typing and spelling errors have been corrected (although some of Rawlings's old-fashioned spellings have been retained as indicative of her idiosyncratic habits). And some consistency has been imposed upon her often irregular spacing.

Blood of My Blood was apparently written, and was submitted for publication, as a novel. Had it been accepted and published in 1929, it would have appeared as a novel—and hence without the notes identifying persons, places, historical events, etc., that are to be expected in modern editions, especially textbooks, of older works of fiction.

Though its readers now may be interested in knowing more about the professors at the University of Wisconsin or the editors of New York magazines who are mentioned by name in *Blood of My Blood*, the book would suffer some loss for the kind of reader for whom it was written by the inclusion of such annotations, either at the foot of the page or at the end of the chapter or of the book. Some of its vitality, as a work to be read as a novel, would certainly be lost. Clearly the latter part of the work is autobiographical, and though the author at least partially conceals the identities of a few characters by giving only the first letter plus a dash for the last name, all the important characters, from the girl Marjorie Kinnan to her Kinnan and Traphagen relatives and ancestors, are fully and, within reasonable limits, accurately identified. In short, the publication now, at last, of this book need not involve its annotation.

ACKNOWLEDGMENTS

I am most of all indebted to my husband, James B. Meriwether, for his encouragement, and for his proofreading assistance and other editorial labors. To the Seajay Society of Columbia, South Carolina, and to its president, Elizabeth C. Havens, I am grateful for access to the *Blood of My Blood* typescript and other Rawlings materials in its archives. Meredith Morris-Babb, editor-in-chief of the University Press of Florida, has been unfailingly patient and helpful throughout the process of bringing this project to fruition, as have the managing editor, Deidre Bryan, and the project editor, Gillian Hillis. And, finally, this book could not have been published without the fine legal advice and dedicated efforts of Steve A. Matthews and Robert O. Meriwether.

Blood of My Blood

PROLOGUE

The physical ugliness of my mother was the bitter drop that tainted the fluid of her life. In her ugliness, she was guilty of the same spiritual inadequacy that so often characterizes beauty: she did not comprehend that the mind and soul, being intangible and therefore more closely related to the eternal, are worthier of service than the eye. She accepted her appearance as a calamity and early decided that the desirable things of this world are those likely to fall to the lot of the beautiful woman: wealth, position, fine raiment and the homage of men.

Her plainness does much to explain her standards. The appalling interlinking of human lives, the one-ness of blood with blood, explain the fiercest gesture of her life—her attempt to impose those standards on her daughter, and to live her daughter's life.

Understanding of her has come to me with time.

Portions of her experiences are universal. Portions are unique. Here is her battle, for herself and for her child; her dedication to false gods; their betrayal of her; the lessons she learned of life and how she learned them.

I offer her story humbly, as a human document.

Blood of My Blood

As a girl of sixteen, Ida Traphagen stood before a walnut-framed mirror in the paternal farmhouse in Michigan and cried bitterly because she was so homely. The tears did not increase her charms. Her face was sharp and angular, with a pointed chin, high cheek-bones, slightly protruding upper teeth, an indeterminately formed mouth of some width, and a long, crooked nose. Her eyes, of a nice blue, were small. When she cried, the lids reddened and swelled almost shut; the nose became red and swollen at the tip; the upper lip swelled entirely out of shape. The spectacle, reflected in the mirror, brought fresh tears, ending with a violent nervous headache to which all her life she was subject.

After the tempest had subsided, leaving only the headache and a profound, resigned melancholy, she would go out to the windmill and pump fresh icy well-water with which to bathe her throbbing eyes and head. The farmhouse was equipped with running water through a home-made piping system, but by the time the water had passed through the pipes in the warm kitchen, its coldness was somewhat expended. She also hoped, by going outside, to avoid her mother; to heal her wounds, as it were, before the pretty, plump, sharp-tongued and stupid little woman could rub salt into them. It took so long for the redness and swelling to subside, however, that Fanny usually came upon her, or called her, before she had recovered from her lachrymose debauch.

"My Lord, Idy, you've been cryin' again. You're the homeliest thing I ever laid eyes on. It doesn't help that long nose of yours to get it red as a beet, and my land, look at your eyes."

The girl looked appealingly at her mother, mute with spent suffering. She had said these things to herself, over and over. The repeated words fell like blows on a heart already numb with pain. She felt them strike and bruise, but she was past bleeding under them.

Her mother's purpose was honest, even laudable. She only wished to point out to her daughter that it was a mistake to make herself more unattractive than was necessary, by indulging in tears. Incapable of delicacy, she relied on the maxim, "Tell the truth and shame the devil." She used the rapier of her tongue without a foil, and not content to make a thrust and cry "Touché!", must make sure that its point sunk deep within the vulnerable flesh.

What would have been the effect on her life, even on her granddaughter's, if Fanny Traphagen had been able to lave her child's aching forehead and sensibilities? She knew why Ida cried. She might have said:

"You are young and healthy, with a fresh, lovely complexion. You have soft, beautiful, chestnut-brown hair. There have been women in history who have gone far, with longer, crookeder noses and higher cheekbones than yours. George Sand was ugly, but she was famous and sufficiently beloved. Your physical appearance is a matter of no import."

But, what would you? She knew nothing of famous women. She had neither read nor heard of them, being glad to read and write a very little, and to hear as history the old wives' tales of her own locality, which had to do with births and deaths and scandals.

She might have said:

"If you acquire wisdom, my child, its white light will transform your plain features. If you acquire beauty of spirit, other souls, attuned to yours, will fly like birds to you and call you lovely."

Not knowing these things, she said:

"I don't know what man will ever want you. It's bad enough for you to look like your poor homely Pa, without taking after his solemn disposition."

The pebble drops in the source water of the shallow stream. Its course is deflected. It goes down this valley instead of that; it meets streams from these mountains instead of those; in a now unavoidable compulsion, the creek must eat its way through sand and thorny areas and never know the rich verdure a few miles away. A certain sort of river, composed of certain elements, arriving by a certain route, flows at last into the eternity of the sea. It is all one to the sea, but who can say that it is a matter of indifference to the river?

Fanny and Abram

There are minds, like soils, incapable of fertility. No amount of enrichment, of cultivation, can produce in them any crop but weeds. Fanny Osmun Traphagen had one of these. Nothing existed for her except the surfaces skimmed by her eyes, blue as cornflowers. Nothing penetrated her head, framed in curls as soft, as golden-brown, as the heart of a chestnut burr, except the casual facts of life and its far from casual conventions. The middle-class virtues flourished in her, their natural milieu, and she passed them on to her children like stern and sacred vessels.

She taught them cleanliness. Ida, her first-born, received the full effect of her mother's horror of the sacrilege of dirt. A house, regardless of circumstances, must be "gone over" every day. It must be "cleaned" once a week, in every crack or crevice, visible or invisible. "Spring cleaning" and "Fall cleaning" were grim gods, on whose bloody altars were sacrificed biannually the peace and comfort of the family and entire nervous equipment of the housekeeper.

She taught them honesty, morality; then threw these desirable qualities into utter confusion by giving them at the same time a wide-eyed reverence for wealth and the material aspects of success, no matter how achieved. Long years later, her daughter Ida was to astonish her own daughter by denying her ethical gods when they came in conflict with her material ones.

Fanny Osmun married Abram Traphagen because he embodied these very ideals. He was clean, honest, and moral, and by the standards of the still pioneer, Michigan community, he was on the way to agricultural success. At sixteen, he had inherited one hundred and sixty acres of partly cleared land from his father. At nineteen he had completed a decent frame house and a red barn, and Fanny, her character as fixed at seventeen as it was to be at seventy, decided that he was the best she could do and married him. She moved into the new house with smug satisfaction; rearranged the few pieces of furniture, made a mental note of what she must soon have in the way of an organ, a plush settee, and a chromo portrait of herself; clamored for a larger vegetable garden past the little white gate in the side yard; planted her own woman's garden of bleeding heart, salvia, cosmos, four-o'clocks, rose geranium and sweet lavender; and began the long business of giving birth to Abram's seven sons and daughters.

Abram adored her. She heckled him, nagged him, lashed him with her flickering little tongue, condescended to play cruel practical jokes on him, such as hiding in the wood on the dark road up which he would come and springing out at his horses with an inhuman shriek, startling them into runaways that gave him once a broken collar-bone. Her perverted humor delighted him. He coaxed her as a middle-aged woman to let down her gold-brown curls and tie them with a red ribbon and bring his lunch to him in the field. Her petite plumpness became plumper, the chestnut curls became soft silver, but she was a pretty woman up to the final day, when the saliva drooled over her chin and the blue eyes glazed at last. Even her children and grandchildren, when most annoyed by her blindness, her prejudices, her mental sterility, loved to look at her.

No one loved to look at Abram, except those who saw his six feet three of weather-beaten gauntness as being beautiful as a gnarled oak deep-rooted in the soil he loved. His shoulders were from boyhood a little stooped with bending over furrows and young plants. His eyes were always a bit a-squint from looking at the sky for weather portents. His step was slow from much weariness, and because one cannot hurry the seasons, or the rain, or the dawn. He walked with the deliberate gait of a very thin elephant and stared ahead of him with the same preoccupation. His solemnity and high cheekbones had about them something of the Indian, with whose Fisher tribe he had much consorted as a lad.

"Abe's half Indian, talks their lingo," his father used to say.

And one of Ida's earliest memories was of an old brave who brought them fish and venison as thanks for trapping on their lakes and streams. She would come down the back stairs in the early morning and find him sleeping in the kitchen, rolled up in his blanket. Abram's grandfather had doctored their horses and repaired their implements, and about the Triphauven family, until the Fishers disappeared, there was a girdle of their wild affection.

Abram did all his work with, to a quicker man, a maddening slowness. He came in from his evening chores almost an hour behind his neighbors; but his chores were better done; the cows milked dry; the plow-horses groomed and their harness sores attended to; their straw bedding was thicker; the hired man was driven to the keeping of cleaner barns and stables.

He ate with inconceivable deliberation, chewing each mouthful of food with the slow gravity of a horse. His great bony jaw swung back and forth, back and forth, and creaked on its hinges. His Adam's apple surged up and down like a slow piston. His hand was knotted and immense. There was a spread of twelve inches between thumb and forefinger, stretched apart, he said, by swinging the axe for weeks on end. When he wrapped his crooked brown fingers around his table knife, or picked up a fragment of meat with them, his hand covered his plate. His joints creaked. When he sat down, his bony knees threatened to cut holes in his trousers. When he lay in bed he made, not a mound under the covers, like Fanny beside him, but a startling array of peaks and valleys and mountains. And Ida looked like him.

His mind, unlike his wife's, was a fertile field denied the blessing of good seed. He could have accepted any knowledge, any wisdom, and reared it to rich bloom. Leisure for reading, for conversation, did not come to him until he was so old that he was puzzled by his very thoughts. He had the barest rudiments of education, schooling being subordinated to his father's need of him, trying single-handed to clear his land.

Ideas only germinated and then decayed in him, like seeds buried too deep to be reached by the sun. He brooded over his ideas. His thoughts were simple and profound. He turned them over and over in his mind, as he ploughed his fertile valleys, cut firewood in his ample forest, harvested his hay and threshed his grain. In the days when he worked of necessity alone, there was not time enough to plant or harvest by the hours of sun, and he planted corn and wheat by the light of a full moon.

He was stretched taut with lean strength, and sometimes cut down a tree before he went to bed. The moonlight was almost his undoing on one of these occasions. The moon threw a heavy shadow, and as the tree fell, it fell within its own shade, and was upon him before his slow eye distinguished tree from shadow. His shoulder was bruised and he lay awake all night with the pain and with his thoughts. He thought about the sun and the moon and about sunlight and moonlight. He wondered why the moon had trickery in it and the sun did not. But the next night he was working again in the moonlight; for it was a part of him, like silver in his veins.

He never accepted the soil as a servant, like his neighbors. It was always mysterious to him. The growth of his apple orchards on a slope above a stream stirred him deeply, but he never spoke of it. He would stand in front of his house, from which he could see on one side, across the road, his full, prosperous barns, and on the other side his own hills and valleys, dipping here to show a deep blue tiny lake, rising here to a patch of timber, on and on until they merged with other men's hills and valleys and the far horizons of Michigan. He would look and brood, and come into the house without a word, inarticulate, thinking, thinking—

He loved the soil. It made him and he made it, like brothers working together. He liked to think about the people from whom he had sprung and who were all dead; his grandfather, a man of property, by name Triphauven, who had come from Holland to New York state and gone west in 1840 to take up government land at a shilling an acre.

His grandfather had had three sons, of whom he loved the two eldest and hated the youngest, Abram's father. The grandfather and the two sons had tricked Abram's father, offering him eighty acres of land if he would renounce his claim on his father's other lands. They would help him clear the land, they said, and since labor was gold, and eighty acres, cleared, would give a man a competence to start with, he agreed and signed away his birthright. They left him to clear the land alone and laughed at him. All his life, Abram was full of old tales that no one wanted to hear.

Ida Traphagen inherited then, if there be such a thing as inheritance, her father's unlovely body and, a greater misfortune, her mother's unlovely mind.

Years of Plenty

Ida May Traphagen was born on the second of January in the year 1868. Her father was then a grave, silent man of twenty, for he had borne alone the burden of his father's undeveloped land for four years. His one brother had given his life to the Union, while Abram, held too young to fight, had not been too young to swing an axe all day, to plough behind a team of oxen, the crude plow tearing at his shoulder blades as it bucked into the tough clods of the virgin land. His father's death merely drove him the harder, so that by the time Fanny Osmun condescended to marry him, he had things in fair shape.

The swamp on the forty-acre plot was almost clear of rattlesnakes, for in cutting marsh grass as winter fodder for his stock, he had killed them by the hundreds. He wore heavy hide boots, home-cured, and as he slaughtered the reptiles expertly with a heavy stock or with his scythe, they could at most sink their fangs ineffectually against his well-sheathed, lanky legs.

When Ida was born, he was raising, for his own use and for market, potatoes, corn, wheat, rye. He was one of the first growers in the state to find money in beans. By the time his eldest-born reached the age at which prosperity was first to assume importance in her life, he was, as farmers go, moderately well-to-do. His barns were good and sheltered a herd of a dozen milch cows and his own bull; several work horses, two of them of sufficient beauty to serve, when not overworked, as carriage horses.

Ida the child was standing beside him one day as he poured buttermilk from the fresh churning into a trough accommodating two dozen squealing, thriving hogs.

"When I was a boy," he said to her, "my father had to keep his hogs in a pen under a lean-to at night, to keep out bears and wolves. They didn't look like these. They had long sharp noses and ran wild in the forest, until we brought them in at the end of summer to fatten them up for the fall slaughtering. We hunted them out with dogs and drove them in, or cornered them and trussed them up and brought them in on the stone-boat."

He waved his gangling arm at the hillside where a flock of sheep cropped the turf or rested under the hickory trees.

"Sheep never paid my father," he said. "Bears got them. But the wool was good on the few he could save each year and brought a good price when he took it in to Detroit."

"Did he stay at a hotel?" the girl queried.

"Well, yes, but I guess you'd call it an inn. On the outskirts of town, and then drove in to Detroit early in the morning."

The girl was not imaginative, but she was faintly stirred by the picture of her grandfather driving all that distance and ordering dinner at a tavern.

"Id-y! Id-y!"

Her mother's voice invariably shrilled out in demand when Abram gossiped too long with anyone, even his own children. The girl hurried back to the house, carrying the empty pails to be washed.

"My land, Abe's slow enough without standin' around gabbin'. What was he talkin' about?"

"About Grandpa's hogs and sheep and going to Detroit."

Complacent little Fanny wiped the perspiration from her forehead, where her curls lay softly damp.

"Your Pa's yarns won't buy you any silk dresses," she commented.

Ida's interest in her father's tales cooled. Pa was awfully slow. Fanny's tongue, like a thin knife, had again sliced into the tenderness Ida felt for her father.

"If you love me as I love you, no knife can cut our love in two."

But Fanny's tongue could do the trick.

That evening a light gig rolled down the dusty roadway past the Traphagen house. In the twilight a handsome, youngish woman, gaudily but shabbily dressed, could be seen sitting stiffly, holding the reins. Fanny was putting the younger children to bed, the hired girl was rattling the last of the supper dishes, and Abram and Ida were picking bugs from the love-apple vines in the garden. They straightened up to stare at the passerby.

"Now I believe that was MacHenry's girl," Abram remarked cautiously. "I shouldn't think she'd show her face in these parts."

"Who is she, Pa?"

"Well, I oughtn't rightly to mention it to a young girl, Dide, but she became a camp-follower during the war."

He straightened his great bent frame and stared into space.

"Squire MacHenry," he mused. "His flute was the first music I ever heard. We called him 'Squire' because he had book-learning and used to settle disputes in this vicinity. He used to go to Fentonville and Holley and get his little brown jug filled with whiskey, and by the time he got home again, he was drunker than fifteen uneducated men. He used to lie down to sleep it off before he got home, in some woods where my cornfield lies now, under a tree, sleeping so sound some boys once took the pants right off him, for a joke. He woke up naked and sneaked home after dark. Then he got him a little white dog that he had to the day of his death, and nobody could get near MacHenry while he slept.

"He played the flute the sweetest of any music I think I've ever heard. Fanny and I went to a traveling opery in Flint once, but it didn't seem to me the music was as sweet as MacHenry's. My father and I were alone here, and when MacHenry got opposite our clearing he'd begin to play his flute. It was his way of saying 'Howdy'. I never heard a bird so sweet, nor no woman sing so sweet, as MacHenry on his flute. It seemed to me I could hear it sometimes when he wasn't there, as if he'd left it behind him in the trees."

His face was tender with the memory of beauty flowing past his ears. The light faded as he turned, embarrassed, to the sharp young features so like his own, watching him with a critical lack of understanding.

"Pshaw," he apologized. "MacHenry was a worthless man."

"His tunes didn't buy his girl any silk dresses, did they?" she asked smugly.

He pinched her cheek and smiled tolerantly at the familiar phrase.

"Babe, you've been listening to your mother," he answered.

Oddly enough, it was MacHenry's girl who gave Ida her first sight of silk dresses; silk dresses, that is, of the world, as distinguished from her mother's "best" dress which hung in sacred folds in a dark closet. The woman had come back to Fenton to live, and when she prospered she drove in and out of town in a fashionable delirium of bustles and long gloves.

Ida puzzled over the anomaly of wickedness combined with, even producing, success. She agreed with the matrons at the sewing bees, who talked too freely, that it was a shame and all wrong. They all meant the same thing. They were honestly horrified at the woman's life; and they were fiercely, bitterly, envious of the material fruits of it.

Fanny saw to it that Ida had nice clothes during the years of plenty, although on one occasion Ida and Flo found it necessary to share a pair of gloves. One wore the right and the other the left. The left-over hands were simply tucked behind them. The other children were too young yet to need other than the simplest frocks, but Ida, who drove four miles to Fenton to school and mingled with the town people, needed good alpacas and merinos and a little fur tippet.

"My Lord, Idy, if it did any good to dress you up," her mother wailed, "but you're almost as humbly in a new dress as an old one."

But there is a picture of Ida at sixteen, nevertheless, in the finest of black moire silk, a gold brooch at the throat, garnet earrings in her ears, and her hair frizzed over her high forehead in stylish bangs. The wide thin mouth is there, with the shapeless upper lip; the long crooked nose; the small eyes. But there is a look of youth and health—she had a clear, rosy skin and soft, shining hair—and it is pleasant to think that there must have been intervals in her plainness when she was not unattractive, and when the blight of her deprecatory self-consciousness was not choking her so that sometimes she could not swallow.

Ida's Men

It is ironic that of the three men who admired Ida Traphagen, she passed lightly over the only one who in due time would have been able to give her the material luxuries she craved.

As a girl of seventeen in her last year at the Fenton High School, she was stopped at the desk of the principal, Mr. Kinnan, as the class filed out for the noon recess.

"I was asked to give you this," he remarked loudly enough to be heard by a dozen pupils. His eyes were twinkling. A dozen heads turned in curiosity as he handed her a thick photograph of the 1885 era.

The photograph was a faithful representation of a local youth, Henry X——, dressed in long skin-tight bicycle breeches, short jacket and round cap of the type since worn by organ-grinders' monkies. He was pictured standing by the side of his new bicycle, vastly wheeled, and the tendering of this token, even through the indirect medium of the school principal, amounted almost to a declaration.

The pupils tittered. The mobile lips of the principal were twitching. Ida blushed. In a beautiful girl, her blush would have been ravishing. It mounted in a soft wave of rich pink and curled into the roots of her hair like sea-shells swinging with the tide. All three of her admirers always found it immensely appealing.

She was suffering acutely, only slightly flattered. She had no idea that Henry, bashful, blue-eyed, a youth of no particular consequence, "had his eye on her." Given her in this public manner, what might have seemed a compliment under more auspicious circumstances, took on the aspect of a joke at her expense.

She settled Henry once and for all by shrugging her shoulders contemptuously and slapping the photograph between covers of a book. The fierce courage with which all her life she arose to an emergency, gave her strength to face down the pack. She tossed her head.

"Let him keep his bicycle and his breeches to himself," she snapped.

The leering boys and girls shrieked with delight at the sally. There was a slapping of thighs and a wiping of eyes with skirt corners. The remark was passed about all over Fenton, and added considerably to her prestige as a wit. Years after, it was told of her, "Why, when Ida was a girl, she used to be perfectly killing."

The appreciative laughter of her audience gratified her immensely. It is to be regretted that she did not take her life's cue from such episodes and see in the *bon mot* a satisfying substitute for beauty; the facets of the mind more brilliant than those of the diamonds that Henry's wife was later to wear.

She took the photograph home and dropped it with casual irritation in the red plush album. Long after, on a visit home with her young daughter, she came across the picture again. The youth's bicycle had become the most expensive of limousines; his breeches were now London-tailored; the photographer's background of canvas curtain was now a background of fine homes, servants and "trips abroad". She was totally unable to reconcile the despised youth of a generation before with the rich manufacturer of her today. They were two different beings. Somewhere the boy Henry, gawky, diffident, must be turning objectionable furrows of soil, like her father. The man Henry had grown up from someone else.

She tried to go back twenty years and imagine herself accepting Henry's photograph graciously; Henry approaching her and asking her to drive to Flint with him in a hired rig to a picnic; Henry proposing marriage; herself accepting; Henry's founding the business that was to make him rich; herself presiding over the near-mansion in which he lived, wearing jewels—the picture dissolved into thin air, for the thing was unimaginable. Nothing fitted in with the photograph of the boy standing by the bicycle.

Would she have encouraged him if she had sensed that he had success within him? She did not honestly know, but thought she might have. It would not have been that she would have married him for his prospects, but simply that she would have seen him with different eyes, glamorous with material achievement. Her daughter saw her sitting with the open album in her lap, staring into space, trying to weave the halo of wealth about a little round monkey cap.

She was unable to dissociate a personality from its material surroundings.

She was equally blind when her best friend, Maggie R—, plump, pretty, popular, married a great gawk of a country boy in whom the wise, or the cautious, would almost certainly have seen genius bursting out in gaunt strength, even as his great frame was bursting out of his shabby clothes. Ida wept and pleaded with her friend not to marry him. Maggie stared at her.

"But I like him," she said.

In the same visit home that brought to light the photograph of Henry, Ida stopped in to visit Maggie. Her friend took her to call on her husband in his palatial offices, where, a nationally revered figure as a surgeon and diagnostician, he dispensed wisdom and beneficence. He bent his huge bulk gravely in salutation to the friend of his wife's youth, took her scrawny hands tenderly between his two paws. The same profundity in the eyes of the man had been in the eyes of the boy; he spoke in the same hesitant accents of his youth; but behind him now were mahogany panelings, the ringing of many telephones, and the patter across deep-piled carpets of the white-clad feet of a dozen nurses and secretaries.

"Well, Maggie," Ida smirked as they left the offices, "I was wrong about him."

Maggie stared as uncomprehending as when Ida had railed against the man twenty years before.

✕

Ida Traphagen appealed to Jay Conrad with the paradoxical appeal of the undersexed woman for the oversexed man. Her frigidity was a challenge. The fact that her *maigre* body was not worth the having, was of no moment in a locality where very little female beauty was to be had at best. She was reserved, dignified with an awkward dignity, in a region where giggles marked the gauche. Her father was generally respected, in a time when contact with the soil was more honorable than today, and altogether she bore for Jay the vague symbolism of a lady. All her life she displayed to those who did not know her well, a calm coldness, the sense of personal integrity, that gave her the distinction of marble.

But there were no revealing turns of light, no veins of warm pink or cream, to give beauty to the stone. She always managed to disappoint people, who felt vaguely that there should be more body to her fierce nobility than they were ever able to discover. Her aura of power was the power of her pride, the last desperate stand of her ego against her self-humiliation.

Jay Conrad was a sport. He was a brown sort of man, sleek and glossy like a chestnut, slightly rotund. He had brown, delighted eyes, full of a naive sophistication. He was two or three inches shorter than Ida, which increased his respect for her. He dressed in browns that contrived to be startling; brown plaid suits, bright tan shoes and gloves, faun bowler hat. He drove a light brown, fast little mare from a cream-colored trap.

He had a good income from vague sources, and was often absent from Fenton two weeks at a time. He sold lightning rods and negotiated land deals. There was talk of horse-trading, of gambling in other cities. One night his rig was seen the other side of Holley, going like mad. He was accompanied by a woman in a red hat, who held her muff in front of her face. It was believed to be Pamela MacHenry.

Ida first came to Jay's attention under the glamor of the Fenton Ladies' Band. The Ladies' Band was smart, it was daring; only the social standing of its members prevented it from being shocking. Ida was being boarded for the heart of the winter, purely as a favor, by the Ed Forte's, a young couple who boasted the social leadership of the town.

For two years, Ida had walked or driven the four miles to Fenton to school, in driving snow or sleet or in rain that moulded her full skirts wetly against her lean limbs. When Abram allowed her to take a horse and buggy in inclement weather, she hitched her rig under a low shed adjoining the school building, and dried or thawed herself at the red-hot round-bellied stove at the rear of the school room.

As her junior year in high school ran into November, it became apparent that the winter would be a bad one. There was a near-blizzard on Thanksgiving Day. One of Fanny's enormous turkey gobblers had been killed and dressed three days before, twenty-eight pounds of ripening succulence, and hung in the store-room over the woodshed off the kitchen. When Lulu the hired girl, half-wit daughter of a less prosperous farmer, was sent up for the bird after breakfast Thursday morning, she found it frozen stiff. She was heard delighting herself by thumping the steely carcass against the rough deal walls. The Hubbard squash, piled snugly in baskets in the same room, were nipped but not injured. The hickory and black walnuts in their sacks were chill pellets, the crisp snow-apples were scarlet frost-bitten cheeks.

The Traphagen family, including a dozen aunts and uncles and cousins, sat in the midst of Michigan bounty while a Michigan storm beat at the windows. Steam and savours rose from the long table with its four-yard white tablecloth; incense of roast fowl, of stuffing, of boiled young onions swimming in butter, of squash and sweet potatoes and raised rolls, starchily redundant; of cranberry jell; of mellow thick coffee drowned in waves of golden cream; of the long array of plum pudding, mince and pumpkin pies, gooseberry tarts, pound cake and layer cakes, that made up the insult of dessert.

Green cord wood popped in the open grate stove in the dining room. Abram burned wood greener than his neighbors, because he liked the alive sound of it.

He chewed his last mouthful of food, no more deliberately than the first. He was the bountiful patriarch who had fed this multitude, but he surveyed the remains of the feast with detachment.

"Babe," he said to Ida, "you won't get as good cooking as your Ma's, but you'd better plan to board out in Fenton the rest of the winter. It's hard on the horses, and I suppose it's hard on you, traveling back and forth in bad weather. I must say I don't think much of the looks of the winter. I don't remember snow on Thanksgiving one year out of ten."

"That's right, Pa," complained Fanny, "Idy's my best help, so send her away from me."

"Why damn it, woman," he snapped, stung as by a wasp, "you put me up to it your very self. You said last night in bed, it was time for Dide to have advantages if she was ever going to have them in time to do her any good. When it stormed today, I thought that would settle it."

Fanny emptied the leftover contents of three cream pitchers into one, scraping out the yellow paste with her chubby forefinger. The process would have been revolting but for what one knew was the immaculacy of her hands.

"I could say Idy needed advantages and still fuss because you sent her away from me," she agreed calmly. "Let her go, don't think about her poor Ma with nothing but a half-wit hired girl to help her. Advantages won't make her any prettier, but maybe she'll learn to appreciate her good home."

The woman was infuriating. She could argue around Robin Hood's barn with utter irrelevancy. Abram was too replete to quarrel with her, to do more than arise and jam an apple log viciously into the stove. He was still madly in love with his wife, but even his untrained mind was aggravated past endurance by her tricks.

"I can help you, Ma," offered Flo. "I can do lots of things Idy does."
Ida choked back her tears.

"The Forte's don't think I'm so dreadful," she protested. "They've asked me why my father and mother didn't let me board with them this winter. I could come home Friday after school, if Pa would send a rig for me, and help Ma bake Saturday."

"Huh!" Ethel snorted. "I'd like to see anybody stop me from going any place I wanted to, if I was as old as Ide." Ethel was the beauty of the family, proud and always belligerent, even when life had beaten her to her knees and made her cry for mercy. In maturity, licked to the point of whimpering, she could toss her head in her embattled moments and defy the universe.

Dell beat the edge of the table with a teaspoon, already impatiently away, riding the steeds of his mind to far, romantic places. From boarding the winter in Fenton, it was only a step to Oregon, to Alaska, to the gold fields, where indeed his destiny awaited him.

Clarence stared moodily at his sister. He loved her, and in his deep-grained melancholy wondered whether she, or anyone else, could find anything but futility, even in Fenton.

"Everybody et too much," grinned Liew, wrinkling his long nose impishly.

✄

Ida boarded two winters with the Forte's. They made much of her, and Fanny Forte took delight in imposing a measure of sophistication on the fresh-skinned country girl who made such killing remarks. Ida basked in their favor, in the excitement of the small-town social life. The stimulation kept a bright blue sparkle in her narrow eyes and an exquisite flush in her high-boned cheeks.

Fanny gave her a silver-gray poplin for Christmas and had her own dressmaker make it up. Ida had to buy artificial bosoms to give her the proper figure under the tight basque, a practice she continued all her life to conceal her emaciation, and to which subterfuge she added from time to time bustles, rats, transformations and switches, all calculated, hoping against hope, to add charm. Concealment always. The pitiful defense of concealment. Her courage, her will to battle, involved her always in a marshaling of her ragged forces against facts.

The silver-gray poplin gave her audacity the night the Fenton Ladies' Band met for practice at Fanny Forte's. All young women of the period played a little and painted a little, and when a new member was to be added to the band, the question was raised, not of her ability, but of her social standing.

It had been decided that the bass tuba was to be added to the orchestration, and that Mag Gunning, Fanny's sister, should play it. The new and shining instrument was unwrapped from its Detroit coverings, and Mag put her lips to the opening. No sound came. She was unable to produce more than the effect of a whistle in a dumb waiter shaft. It was preposterous that so large an instrument should be so silent.

"Why Mag," Ida protested, "anybody could play that."

In jest, she seized the tuba and puffing up her cheeks until her eyes were slits, produced a tremendous bass blast.

The Fenton Ladies' Band shrieked with mirth. Ida was just too perfectly funny. She was so thin and the tuba was so fat. She looked like a thin Chinese girl when she blew her cheeks out and her eyes shut. Ida must play it. She must learn, in time for the next performance, at the Town Hall, the not too well-timed BOOM-boom-boom that was to add "body" to the thin female pipings and treblings of cornet, violin, flute and piano.

Ida was the center of attention. She blushed intriguingly, she tossed her head roguishly. She narrowed her eyes in an attempt to look shrewd and knowing.

Life was suddenly rich with promise. Perhaps, if she could have good enough clothes and live in a city and know rich people, she might overcome the disgrace of being homely and coming from a farm. Somewhere, she knew, there were brighter lights and gayer folk even than this; festivity and shining carriages and hotel life; the theatre, wealth, handsome men adoring beautiful women; something whose name had begun to seep, like a malarial vapor, to Mid-west towns, "Success".

At the "social evening" following the band concert at the hall, Jay

Conrad staked his claim. His attentions were not altogether creditable, a little too shady. But he was of the world, and there was something there—something she wanted.

She despised him for the very reason that he was infatuated with her. He must have bad taste, or he would not have singled her out. He must not be as successful as he seemed, or he could have better. He would not live in Fenton. He would not grasp eagerly at week-end invitations to the Traphagen farm, and smack his lips with such unworldly gusto over the Traphagen dishes.

The broiled quail, garnished with parsley, was finer than that served in the Detroit hotels. Ida laughed at him. The Traphagen melons, cooled in the deep-pitted ice-house, were superb. The pink-skirted mushrooms that Fanny gathered in the meadow where the cows grazed, with Mabel pulling at her skirt and trying to jump on as many as possible, were a great French delicacy, he assured them, (as were the frogs' legs which Fanny cooked grumblingly, throwing a large portion to the dog) and he had even seen them sold in Kansas City in glass jars.

"I suppose some of these things are harder to get, in foreign lands," agreed Abram gravely. "I suppose we take a great many good things for granted, when they come easy. When I was a boy, our wild hogs used to root up a queer vegetable my father called the artichoke. He said his father knew it in Holland and France, where it was much esteemed."

"Oh, Pa!" frowned Ida. Couldn't he see that Jay was a jollier? It made him ridiculous, to fall in so solemnly with Jay's nonsense.

It was now Jay's cream-colored trap which as a matter of course brought her home on Friday afternoon and called for her again on Sunday evening. He always drove through town at a fast clip which embarrassed the girl as much as it gratified her. The hooves of his mare's little feet struck fire from the stones, and the thin metal spokes of the rubber-tired wheels spun themselves into flat disks of light. He bore down on his destination like a fire chief, checking the mare at the last moment so fiercely that she reared high and back-stepped, to ease the hurt on her mouth. Then, with exaggerated gallantry, Jay handed Ida to the ground, or sprang up the steps to rap impudently on the window through which a moment before she had been watching for him, half contemptuously.

It was Jay who followed the Ladies' Band to Detroit and Flint when it made its startling incursions into city concert-giving. The novelty of the sedate group of young ladies, in their respectable basques and jet earrings, squeaking and drumming and booming conventional band music, always drew an audience. The proceeds, above the "expenses" for train fare and bills at bug-ridden small hotels, went to such honorable ends as the new opera house, the public fountain and watering trough.

Jay beaued her vigorously, and she was one of the few members of the band to receive stiff bouquets like funeral pieces. He took her to dinner at better hotels than those the band patronized, and teased her unmercifully at her pronunciation of strange dishes. She tossed her head. But when she was alone again, she stared in the mirror and cried herself into a headache. It was hopeless—. The next time Jay took her to dinner she was more acutely self-conscious than ever. Only her indomitable spirit made her see it through, assuming a stiff dignity that was her nearest approach to ease.

She was willing to suffer thus, for she saw the faintly shabby cosmopolitan life to which Jay introduced her, as the door that might lead to other things. She practiced walking, posturing, rising and sitting, and achieved in this also a strange inflexibility that was almost patrician.

She enjoyed him most when they had no audience to embarrass her and before whom he must show off. He was a little humble, alone with her. He never attempted further familiarity than squeezing her ungloved hand one cold night, under the buffalo robe. She rebuked him merely by placing her hands outside the robe, where the frost chilled them to a most unamorous stiffness. He was on the verge of a "declaration" again and again, held off by what neither of them recognized as her own indecision as to what she wanted of him.

Then, one Sunday evening in a chill winter twilight, he drove up to the Traphagen farm to find the rig of Mr. Kinnan, the school master, hitched to the post in Jay's accustomed place. He sat staring at it a few minutes, then wheeled the mare about and whipped her back to Fenton. He never again came closer the house than to drive by and lift his tasseled whip in greeting. He spoke to Ida in Fenton's social life as a casual acquaintance. But there was always in his bright brown eyes the look of a dog that has been struck and sent home.

As a chubby middle-aged man, degenerated into a small hotel keeper, he was to astonish Ida's daughter with the wistful look of claim that he laid gently on the gaunt woman.

Mr. Kinnan

Surely a cross-section of her personality is revealed in the fact that for nearly two years after marriage, Ida Traphagen found it almost impossible to call her genial husband anything but "Mr. Kinnan". There is a congenital physical coldness in it, an enslavement to convention in the respect for his position which it indicates, and a glimpse of the motivating force of her life: her ambition, the fierce urge of the mediocre to rise above the commonplace, an urge so vital that it endowed her with its own distinction.

"Mr. Kinnan" was the new principal of the Fenton high school, and after Asbury, the superintendent of schools, the intellectual arbiter of the small community. Behind his twenty-eight years, which seemed to sit on him with buoyant humor, lay unguessed-at travail. There was a grimness in pursuing an objective that only occasionally hardened the lines about his sensitive mouth.

Overcome with her respect for him, there was yet almost nothing about him of which the country girl approved. His all but tragic past was an intense irritation to her. He was not a man to boast of difficulties overcome, but if occasion brought any of the facts of his early life into the conversation, she fretted, suffering, until the subject was changed. Its principal disgrace lay in its poverty. To its nobility she was consistently blind.

When he was sixteen years old, Arthur Kinnan saw his father flash out beyond the horizon of life. A most passionate man, a most fiery man, he had given his passion and fire to the service of the Lord, as had his sires and his wife's sires before him. Because he questioned the service—an early letter tells of his first conducting of a revival, and says that very few had come to the mourners' bench—his spirit had not been strong—"Someway I feel that I failed to move them"—he flagellated himself into a fiercer consecration.

His own household was savagely religious. But at the table, and in the daily life, there was beauty of speech and grace of thought, a preoccupation with high matters. On the table, and on the backs of his eight children, was almost nothing.

At sixteen, Arthur Kinnan, acknowledging for God only the beauty of the physical world, for Maker only the creative life force surging through it, turned his back on the Jehovah of Methodism, his father's master, and took up the more immediate matter of supporting his father's offspring.

He did manual labor, and his wages fed them. He came home whistling from a day in the sand-pit of an Ohio brick kiln, to play a softer father to Madeline and Grace, to Luella, to Will, to little Edith Wilmer and Marjorie. Mabel had been sent to Aunt Annie, but the rest clung together, taking life too seriously and food and raiment too lightly.

At night the boy studied, sometimes burning his candle until it was extinguished by the dawn. There was no smugness, no unseemly earnestness. It was simply that he came of generations of men who had been scholars, and one learned as much as was humanly possible, as a matter of course. An advanced education was the foundation of his future life. He planned for it with the same instinct by which a bee prepares the comb for the honey. And it was mere fortuity that a fragile, exquisite, dream-living mother and six children must be fed meanwhile.

He was some years late in entering college. When he finally set off for Michigan State college, the old M.A.C., with a parcel of lunch and a green carpet bag, his father's babies were children; the children, grown. They watched him drive off, adoringly, waving to them from the Christian neighbor's buggy that would take him to the station. He was some blocks down the dusty street, when he saw a small figure pounding desperately after the buggy. It was Willy, bringing as offering his first savings. In moist, sweaty silver he had six dollars.

At college, Arthur went his way with the lack of distinction of the adult student. He built himself a one-room shack on the outskirts of Lansing and lived principally on unleavened bread that he made himself. He was nervous, tall, thin, with black hair and too-wise gray eyes. He walked with a long stride with a little hitch in it, his head thrown back, his arms swinging free. He was totally un-self-conscious. A riotous sense of humor and an excitement for the beauty of life that was like an appetite, carried him with sanity through nightmares of privation.

A Lansing woman who stumbled on his mode of life, smuggled cakes and puddings into his shack in his absence. He had almost finished with college before she revealed herself. She had wit enough to know that any man other than an eccentric who would live thus, would prefer his own heavy bread to that leavened with pity.

He graduated *cum laude*, without loss of dignity or humor. As a bachelor of science, other degrees must wait while he picked up again the financial burden of his father's family. Teaching was the logical first step. Time brought him to Fenton as principal of the high school. Within a few days he had selected the unwitting Ida as his wife.

He chose her because, in contrast to the high-strung intellectuality of the women of his family, she seemed healthy and normal. He could not see her material desires undermining that normalcy. In contrast to the circuit riding of his youth, she seemed a link with something stable, with the thing he loved above all things—the land. The land to him meant beauty and peace and permanence. He did not know until too late that she hated it.

The well-ordered bounty of her mother's house represented to him the art of living. He longed for order and for bounty. How was he to know that the girl belonged to that sect of women who make a fetish of order, and of bounty a display? Life to him was to be taken jovially and beautifully, no matter what its outcome. To her, the outcome was so vital that joy and beauty had no place in it, for very irrelevance. Her sole qualification to be his wife was her courage.

The psychology of mis-mating awaits an analyst. No check has been made of destinies altered by its torments. Yet in the end it seems likely that there is not, after all, so much divergence of course that can be traced to any mis-fitting of lives. The personality is too complete, the ego too ensheathed. Marriage is too superimposed a bond to make much difference to the essential "I" within. Certainly the essential Ida and the essential Arthur, totally unsuited to consummate each other's happiness, managed to live a peaceable common life, yet, mentally and spiritually, to go their separate ways. Of what import is a change of residence when the mind and soul continue to occupy the same apartments?

The school teacher's acceptance by the country girl was a foregone conclusion. His prestige was enormous. There was no wealth in the town, to establish social standards disparaging to his position. His personal charm was irresistible. His "future" was believed to be assured. He was studying law. There was no reason why he might not become a congressman, a senator, a judge, the President. Abe Traphagen was gravely flattered by his visits. Humbly, he entered into conversation with the young principal while his daughter helped her mother serve the dinner. Mr. Kinnan excited him. For days after he had been there, Abram had ideas to mull over in his mind.

The thought of refusing him scarcely occurred to Ida. But she withheld her approval of him, from the start. Back of her immense respect for him, her admiration for his capabilities, was an instinctive mistrust. He lacked even the worldliness of Jay Conrad. He laughed so boisterously. And on the fringes of his life hung that dreaming, impractical mother; those wide-eyed solemn sisters who studied so voraciously, and whose clothes still bore traces of charitable Methodism.

Mr. Kinnan was unaware that Ida had a "steady beau". He stopped her after the history class on Friday, and as simply as though he were assigning a lesson, said:

"Miss Traphagen, I should like to call on you at your home on Sunday evening."

Her quick blush swam over her face. Sunday evening belonged to Jay. It was the evening that belonged to any couple with an "understanding".

Mr. Kinnan's eyes twinkled.

"In fact, Miss Traphagen, I should like all your Sunday evenings, from now on."

She balanced the two men in an instant. She skimmed over the possibilities of both lives. And she plunged into the uncharted seas before her, a swimmer without fear. Always, under her awkwardness, her self-doubting, she had the courage to seize the moment.

"Very well, Mr. Kinnan," she said stiffly, inclining her head. She turned away as seemingly calm as though such precipitate overtures were common. The young principal was delighted. She was seventeen, but starkly mature.

There was a two-years' informal engagement. Neither had the opportunity to change the preconceived conception of the other.

One August evening Mr. Kinnan drove up to the Traphagen farm-house in his hired rig, after some weeks' absence.

The country was golden in the late sunlight. Abram's wheat fields were sifted over with a golden dust. The windows of the square white farmhouse were blazing with the reflected sun. As Mr. Kinnan drove up, the interior seemed to be on fire. He was about to take a wife from this golden place, from this brown soil. She would bring its stability with her, its yellow sun, its Michigan richness.

As he drew Ida behind the folding doors of the double parlor, with is chill, immaculate odor, and seated her on the green plush sofa, she knew why he had come. She was ready.

"Ida, I'm going to Texas to teach, at a better salary. There will be a position in the school for my wife. We could save enough money to start me in law. Will you go?"

He might have said Timbuctoo. It was all the same. She did not love him; she was incapable of romantic or sexual love. He was offering her hard work instead of the life of a lady. But he was a rung in the ladder that surely must lead somehow, some time, to a patrician living. Life must compensate her, somehow, for the long nose, the narrow eyes, the gauche body; for Abram's farm; above all for Abram's farm. Out of Michigan into Texas. What did the place matter? It was all on the way. Beyond the horizon was splendour.

She nodded her head. He took her by the shoulders. A moment of misgiving seized him. Did he not, after all, need a woman of fire? But his father and his mother had been made of fire; and they had only begot poverty and death and hungry children. He put such desires forever behind him. He had chosen peace, and would make life yield him beauty.

"Ida, do you love me?"

She smirked a little. A phrase from a novel came to her.

"I think, in time, I can learn to care for you."

The answer was modest and stable. He frowned slightly and let it pass.

They were married on a hot August night in 1887. Ida helped her mother in the kitchen until noon. She bathed in cold water in the copper bathtub and dressed in the starched embroidered muslin of her bridal underwear. Flo and Ethel helped her, and Mabel clung to her skirts and cried. Ida was going to Texas. It was like death in the house. Flo was complacent, knowing that marriage comes to all good girls who wait. Ethel was envious of the burst for freedom.

When Ida was dressed, in the gray silk moire that was both wedding and traveling dress, she slipped alone into her mother's room to look in the longer mirror. What would Mr. Kinnan think, if or when he discovered the artificial bosoms, layer on layer of starched ruffles? When he did, he burst into unseemly laughter. How could she use a curling iron on the train? When her bangs were not frizzed, she was a sight.

She was a sight anyway, she decided, and stared morbidly at her features until the tears began to swim from her eyes, her nose reddened, her upper lip swelled, and as Fanny announced complacently to the guests, was a treat to look at, by the time the ceremony was performed. The friends, relatives and neighbors sat tight-packed in parlor, dining room, and hall. Little girls in white dresses pinched one another and were sent outdoors, where they raced and screamed. Abram trembled and gave the bride away and cleared his throat and rattled his lank joints. He pinned his gift on his daughter of a fleur-de-lis watch set with turquoises. Fanny swished a palm-leaf fan back and forth and hoped audibly that Idy wouldn't come running home with a pack of young uns.

Marriage and Texas

At nineteen, it was impossible for any young woman to do other than take Texas, as well as marriage, as an adventure. There were disagreeable aspects to both. But Ida was outbound on the high road, and she indulged herself in the conviction that all would be well.

Big Springs was a prosperous pioneer town with an immense respect for book larnin'. Nothing was too good for the fine young school principal with his dude mustache and his prim wife. At the reception held for them, there was much foot scraping and respectful folding of hands behind the back. Tobacco was chewed with the utmost stealth, cheeks bulged only ever so little, and the earnest ranchmen tiptoed to the door to spit.

The men, the women, the bare frame buildings, starkly unpainted, overwhelmed Ida with their crudeness, but the cloak-laying before her was balm to her soul. Among the raw-boned, wind-burned women, she passed for handsome, for the first time in her life. Her clothes were admired and copied in calico and in Chicago silks.

The community descended on the young couple with a housewarming. There were donations of flour and sugar, of aprons, of cakes, pies, and puddings; a wild-cat hide; and such precious utensils in a town far from supplies, as dishpans and pots and kettles.

The town fiddler, from Three X ranch, had left his fiddle outside the door, and when it was ascertained that Mr. and Mrs. Kinnan were not too God-fearin' for a little music, the fiddle was brought in, and there were reels and jigs and a tremendous stamping of feet. Out of remote Scotch memories Mr. Kinnan produced a Highland fling. The last barrier was down. Young Mrs. Kinnan was induced to promise the other ladies that she would teach them how to paint pansies on plush. They would send to Chicago for materials. The bride was flushed with success.

It would seem that the solution to Ida's life might be always to play this game of big frog and little puddle. But there would always be other puddles, bigger worlds. The insolence of her ambitions would have done credit to a more formidable personality.

From having considered the Texas venture faintly disreputable, she accepted it as quite a clever adventure for young people on the threshold of bigger things. She could always make small talk, she thought, in the life into which she would eventually graduate, of the reception and the housewarming.

She never spoke later, however, of the sun-blistered cheap house on the edge of town, backed up to the appalling prairie; of the Texas blizzards that enveloped them like the white cloak of an avenging angel; of the sandstorms filling every crevice with fine grit; of the tarantulas that sprawled across the thresholds and had to be watched for in the bedrooms.

There were two little prairie dogs who found the way to her pantry. She missed sugar and molasses, and came on them one day, frozen into small tawny statues on an urn, with their paws on the edge of the molasses jug. The cover was ajar and their whiskers were deliciously besmeared.

There was a juvenile rattlesnake who flung himself back and forth across her porch in a childish frenzy, and with his six inches of animation and his mere button of a rattle, would not let her enter her own door. There was, for days, a whirring under her back steps whenever she went up or down, that she took for a locust. "Mr. Kinnan" heard it and probed out a Texas rattler thicker than his arm, coiled to the width of a washtub. In a day when folk very occasionally survived a rattler's fangs, and then only in spite of the cruelty of whiskey added to already stimulated hearts, she had walked back and forth across the literal jaws of death, missing annihilation by the geometry of steps.

They made unconventional friends of a pair of upper-class bachelor ranchmen. They were invited to spend a week at Moody's ranch, miles distant over the cactus-bitten desert. For days Ida baked, in old Michigan style; bread, buns, cake, cookies, pie; roasted the hindquarter of a young sheep; baked pots of pork and beans; put up jars of butter and preserves. The food was partly for their own use on the road, and partly a Michigan boast to a Texas ranch-house.

They hired an old covered wagon in which to make the two-day trip to Moody's ranch. Ida served meals from it, by the side of a camp-fire, with the stiff decorum with which she presided over all of her meals. Arthur's spirits bounded to meet the desert, the burnt-orange sunsets, and opal sunrises. He was hilarious all day as they creaked off their miles of sagebrush and sand; hushed and rapt at night, as the moon swung over the low rise of ground and the coyotes howled from hummock to hummock.

The girl was not afraid. Her fears lay in the twilight regions of human thought and action. Her body she would at any time have exposed to any dangers, perhaps because she despised it so. (There is a story that when she had ripped a pair of blazing curtains from the wall and fears were expressed for possible scars on her hands, she had said, "Yes, I thought of that, and I decided they couldn't be any uglier.") But she whimpered a little as night came down on the Texas desert. It was so desolate. It was the outpost of life, to which a woman ugly enough and poor enough might conceivably be exiled.

When they reached the ranch-house, and the host and his men cheered a greeting from the wide veranda, she was awkwardly coy and gay, for very joy at seeing lights again.

The next day Moody took them in the ranch wagon on a tour of the place. She sat in dignity on the high seat while wolf traps were inspected, the herding of cattle explained. Her husband exploded with enthusiasm.

"How can a professional life possibly compare with this!" he cried, with a sweep of his arm. "Moody, you have freedom and beauty in the hollow of your hands—"

Moody grinned and strolled away to pick a yellow cactus blossom for young Mrs. Kinnan. She clutched Arthur in a panic. It was her first inkling of the madness that was to possess him. She sensed his frenzy, for the very soil itself.

"Arthur, are you crazy! They make money, of course, but you fool, it's only farming after all!"

He listened in astonishment. Then he burst out laughing.

"Oh Moody," he called, "my wife used to be a poor farm girl and she thinks that even ranching isn't quite decent."

"Arthur!" She was on the verge of tears. "We weren't so poor—what an impression to give—"

"Ma'am," remarked Moody, winking at Kinnan, "the life of a ranchman is so indecent that he's almost immune to impressions."

By the time they had circled one border of the ranch, evening thundered down on them, black with approaching storm.

"I should have noticed that sky," apologized the host. "We're in for it. We can't possibly make the ranch-house. Now I wouldn't expose this young bride to a Texas storm for the price of my cattle, and if you can put up with some inconvenience, I'll stow you in the dug-out for the night."

The dug-out was reached by dark, and the young couple put to bed in the wide bunk, its dampness thawed out by a quick fire in the small round-bellied stove. The "ground-hog's hole", as Moody called it, some six feet deep, contained only bunk, stove, two shelves and a chair. Moody went on to the ranch-house. Ida examined the bed for cleanliness, shivered, allowed her husband to coax her into smiling wryly, allowed him, with an air of patient resignation, to caress her, and dropped at once to sleep.

She awoke to find the world flooded. The storm had beaten through the door, down the stove flue and seeped through the very walls. The water reached the mattress of the bunk, and shoes and shirts and petticoats and her limp embroidered drawers floated about, like relics of the Ark. Confronted by utter calamity, she was stoic, even cheerful. She laughed, a little hysterically.

When there came a pounding on the rough wooden door, and Moody's jovial voice inquired whether entrance would be perfectly proper, she primped a bit under the covers and put out a head neat with smoothing. The dug-out was bailed out, a fire started, and hot coffee and hard biscuits served in bed while the clothes were drying.

Moody congratulated the bride on her courage, and not having laid eyes on a personable woman in two years, insisted that she was charming, even in a Texas dug-out. Mr. Kinnan paraded about in too little clothing and discussed ranching with his friend, oblivious to smoke, to wet, and to the smell of drying leather.

But these and other adventures of a frontier community were only told to her children. She sometimes regretted having used them for stories, for fear her son and daughter might tell them again "in public". They didn't matter unless "people" knew about them.

During the years they spent in Texas, Mr. Kinnan was constantly studying. He bought books. They saved money. All was in order that he might "get his start". But in later years, his wife made only the vaguest references to the Big Springs period. "When Mr. Kinnan was engaged in educational work in the Southwest—". The drama of the raw life, its gropings for contact with the civilized world, were never food for thought, to say nothing of being meat for conversation. It was crude and therefore disreputable; shabby, and therefore disgraceful.

In 1894 Arthur passed his Civil Service examinations with a high rating, and was assigned to the electrical division of the United States Patent Office at Washington. He would take his law degree at George Washington and practice Patent Law when they had saved enough more for him to make the break. He was obligated for a portion of his salary towards his mother's support. His brother and sisters were going through the University of Michigan with financial fitfulness, and his life was not yet his own. Ida had heard that Patent Law was highly remunerative. Arthur had heard this too, but he also knew that it was a branch of the law not too exacting as to hours and time. It meant leisure, as well as money, for—other things.

And Washington itself? Ida saw a great bronze door swing wide for her. It framed vistas of society, of wealth, of frock-coated diplomats and gorgeously gowned women walking to and fro in front of the White

House. Among them was a tall, thin, distinguished figure, transformed from a self-conscious Michigan girl into a woman of the world by the sole miracle of fine clothes, dressed hair, manicured fingers and contact with other cosmopolites. She wore a sweepingly trained white satin gown. But even in the vista, it was given its frontal grace through artificial bosoms. Fancy could only go so far.

Washington

Magnolia trees in blossom. Purple wisteria on Rhode Island Avenue. Flags flying from the embassies. Carriages slapping their rubber-tired wheels over rain-wet asphalt. The Leiter's are entertaining again tonight—they are using fifty thousand dollars' worth of American Beauty roses in the decorations. They say that at the last ball, the ballroom was divided in half with a plush rope, one side for the pretty girls, the other for the plain. Mary Leiter herself took her place promptly on the pretty side. They say—.

Push carts of daffodils around Dupont Circle. Memorial Day. Everyone takes daisies and roses to Arlington. Arthur and Ida take some, to be a part of the occasion. A parade on Pennsylvania Avenue. The Marine Band plays in Potomac Park, a little shabby in the shadow of the Washington monument. A reception at the White House. Mediocre people shuffle nervously in and triumphantly out. Ladies, dressed in pink voile of a summer morning, alight from their carriages and sweep daintily through Center Market, their nigger butlers in the rear toting immense pretentious baskets.

"Andrew, come see if this melon is ripe."

Tap-tap. Plunk-plunk. Tap-tap.

"Sho' is 'M. Sho' oughta be sweet and ripe."

Outside, an old negress in an immaculate apron and the dignity of a real hat.

"Lavender, swe-e-e-t lavender!"

The cry is plaintive, like a mourning dove. She is out of her time. This is a sad, haughty city, but it is not sad enough. She should be crying on the steps of Mt. Vernon, or Monticello,

"Lavender, sweet lavender—"

Senators and congressmen sitting in front of one in the clanking street cars. The smell of arbutus in Rock Creek Park. The acrid smell of the Zoo, and the white swans idling on the ponds. The holly tree near the Smithsonian, and the sneaky-faced visitors from the West who steal small sprigs from it. Washington stamps her foot at the intruders. They have paid for her with their taxes but she does not belong to them. She is a woman whose body they have paid for but she only suffers them to gape at her. She will not have them. Be gone! They tiptoe about the public buildings, gaping, and are glad to go home again. The rubber-neck wagons sputter up Connecticut Avenue. The crimson damask draperies of the stone mansions are drawn against them.

The castle on Sixteenth Street. The hundred thousand negroes jammed together in the north-east and south-west sections, and bursting out into side streets and back streets adjoining the avenues. They call for the Monday washing on Saturday, so that they can wear your clothes Saturday night and Sunday. You'd be surprised to see the black bodies shining through your embroidered peekaboo waists. You thought your waists were daring. You should see what black wenches can do with them.

They have Jim Crow cars in Virginia and Maryland, but in the District of Columbia they can sit next to you, if you don't know how to make them move. Uppity niggers, in Washington. What are niggers?

When you come from Michigan, they are only men and women with black hides. You just don't understand. You have to know them better. And when you've known them better, and smelled them and seen their beds, and been lied to and stolen from, you still can't hate them. You still don't understand.

The heat that vibrates from the black asphalt, the asphalt so soft your feet make prints in it. The bare-footed newsboys running whimpering, their feet blistering. "Please Keep Off the Grass". The breathless nights, with the sweat soaking the bedclothes. Anybody who is anybody goes away in the summer.

October days, with the perpetual Washington maples fluttering scarlet wisps to the sidewalks. Massachusetts Avenue, that seems a maze of black carriages discharging long-cloaked splendid women trailing over the carpets under the canopies—or else seems shut-up and altogether deserted.

The musty smell of the public buildings. The water coolers in the halls. The Patent Office, the Post Office, the Bureau of Printing and Engraving, the Navy Building, the Treasury Building—the whole gloomy, underpaid, red-brick network of the Civil Service. The swarms of pale employees rushing in at a quarter of nine, gobbling milk and crackers and Charlotte Russe at noon at nearby dairy lunches, or opening spinsterly packages of sandwiches on the office desks; rushing for the trolleys at five o'clock. And shockingly, even though he is soon to be a principal examiner, among them—"Mr. Kinnan".

$$\mathbf{X}$$

The ten square miles of the District of Columbia have always been dotted with boarding houses. Thousands of small government salaries can reach no further than "Room and Board by the Day or Week". East and north of Eleventh Street, squatting in the rear of the Capitol, around the railroad station, they are dingy, squalid. As one moves north-west, they take on cleanliness and dignity, passing through all stages of gentility to gray stone fronts whose secret you would never suspect.

The boarding house on P Street had been recommended to Arthur and Ida before they moved to Washington. Most formal letters had passed back and forth. Miss Renée would welcome them to her home, to a suite of two rooms in her home. Miss Renée met them at the station in person and payed for the hack.

The two rooms were decorous with green Brussels carpet, black wal-nut furniture, melting wherever possible into gray marble tops. The suite was chaste with starched white curtains, ruffled, looped back to show neat ferns on window-sills. The wash stand was glistening with white porcelain. Over it, and beside the bird's-eye maple dresser, hung calen-dars of sunset scenes, with a wooden receptacle like a bird bath, for matches, and a precise square of sandpaper on which to strike them. There was only one room in the P Street boarding house that had ever suffered the social catastrophe of having matches struck on the wall pa-per. The room had been repapered and the occupant dismissed.

Arthur Kinnan walked briskly into the quicksand of government ser-vice. Only his wife's lack of passion for him could have prevented her stifling with jealousy at the absorption with which he could throw him-self into whatever work was claiming him. He mastered the intricacies of the electrical division of the Patent Office, he studied law at night, attended some classes at George Washington.

He thrilled to the physical beauty of Washington, walking to and from his office, his head thrown back, occasionally whistling to a bird in a park, or making a remark or two aloud to himself. He perceived at once the futility of his government profession and resented from the start the labyrinth of routine.

But each day was beautiful, each day was good. He would build a home in the midst of this beauty, a refuge after generations of itinerancy. Over this would preside the Holland precision of his wife, to make it forever clean and peaceful. He hoped in time, by showing her the absurdity of most conventions and many people, to inculcate in her a sense of humor. He would save money out of his eighteen hundred dollars a year. Prime rib roasts were fifteen cents a pound, with liver thrown in. Eggs were twelve cents a dozen.

He would practice patent law. And then—he would buy land, and more land, over which he might walk to the cooling of his feet and the easing of his soul. In time, he could retire upon it, and never again spend one of God's good days affixing the long scrawl of his signature to documents wrapped in yellow Manila paper and sleazy red tapes.

Ida, hugging her dreams, followed his plans indulgently. Everything was in accord with her own aspirations, until he reached his talk of land. That, she told him, was one of his fool jokes. Hadn't he seen enough grubbing along on land without wanting to get into it?

For a few months she lived in a tremulous haze. Wealth, eminence, success, were visible on every hand. She read the newspaper accounts of social functions, down to the last shred of costume worn by the last wife of a secretary of embassy. She walked religiously through the Smithsonian, the art gallery, the Congressional Library, the Capitol; attended sessions of Congress.

She strolled along F Street, the fashionable shopping thoroughfare, and priced or purchased small items with attempted nonchalance. Always her eyes were alert for people who were "somebody". Sometimes she stopped in an F Street soda fountain and treated herself, with a sense of guilt. Often, on the leisurely walk home to P Street, a carriage with a coat of arms on its door would roll close by her.

To all of us, except the very childish or the very wise, there comes at some time a great disillusionment. That the structure was shoddy, else it would not so have tumbled, does not ease the hurt. It came over Ida one day, in a wave of nausea, that her early fears for herself, forgotten these last few years, had been correctly based. She had built herself a house of cards. She knew, in one blinding flash, that there was no place for her in this glamorous life. There was no niche in the social or official life of the capital ready for her. None here. None, indeed, anywhere.

It came over her that her husband, with all his brilliance, was without the strictly personal ambition that takes men to high places. He was above it, beyond it, just as appreciation of that fact was beyond her. She saw him reaching out, not for glory, but for beauty; not for struggle, but for peace. She had nothing, herself, with which to bring the desired things of life to her. Now she knew that her husband would never achieve the position or the wealth to do it for her.

In the first year of Washington residence, she had been called on by the wives of three other Patent Office examiners; by an elderly eccentric around the corner on Q Street who called on everyone within a radius of six blocks; by a mild little Michigan woman whose husband was a clerk in the Treasury Department.

She began to understand that the social strata of Washington were as fixed as geological ones. Even congressmen and their families were no-bodies, unless they had money and standing on the side. Some day, by a miracle, Arthur might attain to a petty judgeship, a place on the Court of Appeals. It would be small stuff. Her husband was now thirty-five years old. Any small success would come too late. From that moment forward, her relations with him were tinged with her faint antagonism. She despised his philosophy of life. To her it was redolent of failure.

For a week, she was sunk deep in despair. She walked the streets in the driving rain, paced up and down her block at night, when her husband was at his classes, until the policeman on the beat inquired if she were in trouble. She shook her head, wisps of straight hair lank across her face, and walked into the respectable P Street house with the tears streaming down her face. Arthur was at first distressed and then irritated. She refused to talk. She only sat red-eyed on the edge of the bed, staring mournfully at him, as though he had betrayed her.

Then, with the courage so characteristic of her, she bathed her eyes, took migraine tablets for her neuralgia, and found her answer to life— her challenge.

She would bear a child. A girl child. Before this child she would unroll the rosy carpet her own feet could never tread. In this child she would attain the distant places, sweet with sophisticated music and florists' flowers. She would control the girl's associates, her school; she could contrive fine clothes for her. In this radiant city she could see that in the girl's youth she was thrown with the children of the great, who would become her friends.

The theory of pre-natal influence was rife in talk and in the ladies' magazines. She would create the child beautiful and talented. The rest could be managed. She dedicated her body and her mind to the production and development of a daughter who would attain to the only things in life worth while: wealth, position, fine raiment and the homage of men.

Maternity, with the rarest of exceptions, is always sheer egotism. "The child is mine. It owes me life. I have its welfare at heart. I know what is best for it. It must do as I say, because I love it so. Never mind its relation to any life but mine."

Women live their children's lives because they are not able to dissociate them from their own, even when the new personality grows adult. It is never the world's child, a child of the universe. It is "my child".

But this dissemination of one's own life is usually fortuitous. One has a child by sheer accident of nature. Or one decides that it would be pleasant or natural to have a child. There is no scheme, until the circumstance of maternity expands one being into two, and the impulse to live the second life becomes irresistible. In the case of Ida, we see the phenomenon of a deliberate extension of her own life for a deliberate purpose; a deliberate intent to live the new life. A peculiarly ruthless mother love is at work.

Maternity

The actual production of the wonder child was a matter of some little difficulty. It was necessary, in the first place, to trick her husband into paternity.

He had broached the indelicate subject of children before their marriage. He intended to have none. They were too reminiscent of poverty-struck Methodism. He was too loyal to his own even to paint for her the picture of horror brought before his eyes by babies: his father's household, swarming with them, underfed, underclothed, objects of Methodist charity; his ineffectual, dreaming mother dandling them absent-mindedly while she recited poetry to those of them old enough to listen.

He loved them all, as they loved him, as if they were his own offspring. Indeed, it was as though at sixteen he had fathered his brood and was done with paternity. He wanted no more of it. In the eight years of his marriage, he had avoided it by the simple expedient of his own self control; simple to a man who had gone cold and hungry for a purpose. His body was vibrant, strongly emotional; but at will he could shut an iron door against any of its needs.

Ida deliberately detained him against his will.

Twenty years later she was to throw the fact at her daughter as proof of the claim she had on her child. She could not understand the revulsion it occasioned.

Arthur was furious when she informed him blandly that conception had taken place. Her purpose was her secret. He could only attribute the misfortune to the most unexpected passion in a passionless woman. He raged. He saw disorder stalking into his life. He begged of her to inquire of other women if there were not something to be done about it. She laughed at him and narrowed her eyes shrewdly.

"Arthur, it's too late," she said cryptically.

He ran his hands through his black hair, already graying at the temples.

"We'll do the best we can," he said. "But I'm very sorry."

She was not disturbed. The scantiest cooperation was all that she required.

A lesser difficulty revolved around the new home, recently contracted for and begun in the north-east suburb of Brookland. With the recklessness that always seized Ida on the verge of a battle, she had been precipitate at an awkward time. But the doctor could wait for his money. Bess Severance would come on from Detroit to nurse her—Bess, whose capacious bosom had mothered her as a lanky schoolgirl. The new house could be hurried. Perhaps the mortgage could be a trifle higher.

They made frequent trips across town in the slow trolley to watch the building. Arthur so trusted the development of the city that he considered it a toss-up as to which section they built in. He was privately certain that only good could come of any land he bought. But as time went on, it was apparent that he had chosen the cheaper part of town, and that the development in its direction was low-class. As a matter of fact, he had bought his site in the raw suburb because he could get three times as much ground for the same price. On the grounds were immense oak trees. The house was to stand in their shade, under their protection. To Ida, it seemed a little gloomy, but Arthur was enthralled.

As the house took form, and the child's embryo developed, Arthur's native enthusiasm took hold of him. Ida dropped hints as to what the child would be:

A little girl with curly golden hair. A beautiful little girl, with exquisite features and the grace of a fairy. She would have the disposition of an angel. And tucked in the ivory perfection of her throat, would lie a golden voice. She would sing, and the world would be at her feet.

The picture was enchanting. The inherent tenderness of his nature overcame him, and within a few months he was planning as warmly as the mother for the singing flower.

Unproved theories are cruel things to be turned over to the layman. Truth, accepted, is more digestible, for it is riper. Folk saw a feverishly eager young woman sitting alone at concerts. At every musical event of the winter of '95 and '96, she was there, a homely woman, with her long neck thrust anxiously forward from her bony shoulders, listening to the waves of sound with a fanatic's fervor. It was Ida, led pitifully by the doctrine of pre-natal influence. She was absorbing song.

She haunted art galleries, attended lectures. Her strained expression never varied, for it was all without beauty or meaning to her. The child was to be born with an instinct for all these things. The complete irony of it did not become apparent for twenty-five years, when the grown child acknowledged that of all the arts she found painting and music the least comprehensible.

In late May, 1896, the Kinnan's moved into the new home, acceptable even to Ida, in the shade of the oak trees. The furniture was decent enough. Her linens were impeccable. There were lace curtains, a Polar bear rug, a silk scarf draped over the black marble mantel in the double parlor, a settee upholstered in mulberry silk, a reed chair, two gilt chairs for the hall; the Stag at Bay; the portrait of the lion whose eyes followed you; all the up-to-date paraphernalia of the era; and over all the shine and polish of Ida's blood-sweating housekeeping.

She was in a fever of joy, like a professional soldier with the promise of war. The flush on her cheek, the glitter in her eyes, were not Madonna-like but militant. For this brief period in her life, she was not conscious of her own appearance. Her condition was not obvious, as is often the case with long, lean women, but had she been twice as conspicuous because of it, she would still have marched boldly about her business.

On the hot August Saturday of the child's birth, she rode to town in the slow trolley to market, walking the mile from the end of the line to her home with a generous basket of carefully chosen provender. Her discomfort began in the afternoon. Until twilight she paced the floor of her bedroom, fighting her pain. Nurse Bess put her to bed then, where she lay without sound until her delivery, her lips compressed to a thin line, her eyes narrowed in defiance. She would pay a thousand times the price, if need be.

When the soft morning sun flooded her white counterpane, the next day, and Bess came, rotund and affectionate, bearing hot good coffee and later, the child, she felt herself flooded with love, with exuberance, that was a revelation to her. She wanted to crush the infant against her body in a strangling embrace. She was suffocated with ecstasy.

The baby, oddly, had hair on its head at birth. It was black hair, not gold, and it was as straight as a string. The features were not promising. But of course it was too early to tell.

And somehow the dark-haired thing that was like all other infants, took the place of the singing flower with curly golden hair, and was as well beloved. It was assumed that all the charms and abilities of the planned-for child, all save the yellow hair and the beauty, were inherent in this one. It could not be otherwise. It is impossible to determine whether the woman's necessity for miracles from the child was so keen that she shut her eyes blindly to its mediocrities, or whether in all honesty she believed it a superior being. At any rate, her plans went forward.

Mr. Kinnan, for nervous excitement, had the hives.

✕

It is almost impossible for any female infant, if not deformed, to be totally unattractive when immaculately clean and "cunningly" dressed. It is doubtless one of Nature's devices for getting them raised to maturity.

Ida's child was no exception. It was healthy, clean, with the clear blue eyes and rose-petal skin of all normal infancy. Its white leather baby carriage was lined with a symphony of white embroidered ruffles and blue bows. The baby wore real lace and a soft blue broadcloth coat, bordered with otter fur. Pinned inside the edge of the otter-trimmed blue bonnet was a row of artificial curls.

Sentimental women stopped the carriage and exclaimed. Department stores were run on more informal lines in those days, for women in business were still "ladies"; in the Washington shops, salesgirls dropped their customers and flocked around "the darling". Ida's heart swelled to bursting. If she had walked out of the building, around it, and in again, she would often have found the same play being enacted over some other infant with curls, real or artificial.

The Foundation

Ida laid the foundation of her child's life on personal appearance. She remedied the lank thinness of its hair by curling it with hot irons. When it was necessary to take it out in public on a rainy day, she lamented bitterly. She swathed its head in veils, and unwrapped it like some fragile trophy, peering anxiously for vestiges of the curl.

Her first anger at the child burst out when, crisp in white organdie and a small pink sash, it waddled away and sat down in a mud puddle. She shook it viciously. She so impressed it with the enormity of this offense that the girl reached full maturity before she was able to shake off a tense stiffness when in fresh clothes.

At the age of four, minute brown freckles began to appear on the child's nose and cheeks. Ida was frantic. She rubbed its skin raw with lemon juice. Arthur roared with laughter at her, then grew stern.

"You are a very foolish woman, Ida, to risk injuring the child's skin permanently. She will outgrow her freckles, probably, and if she doesn't, what earthly difference does it make?"

She threw him a look of scorn and continued to buy creams and lotions. One day she led the child to him in triumph.

"Now I want you to see for yourself how much Marjorie's skin is improved," she said haughtily. "For the past month I have been using a clear, harmless freckle lotion highly recommended by Woodward and Lothrop."

"I noticed the bottle in the cabinet a month ago," he said quietly. "I emptied out its contents and re-filled it from the faucet. For the past month you have been using clear, harmless water—highly recommended by me."

She drew a quick breath, then without a word dragged her daughter away. The hearty laughter that echoed after her had a sinister sound, like the mirth of demons. She would never tell him, now, how much was at stake. She would fight it out entirely alone.

Such episodes were mere trifles in the path. More serious was the birth of a boy at this time. Being utterly enchanted with his daughter, and delighted to find how little difference she made in the order of the house, under his wife's scrupulous management, Arthur had suggested that a son would complete the family nicely. She had refused.

The advent of the boy was sheer accident. If she had been a religious woman, she would have asked whether God were not punishing her for having taken it upon herself to create her daughter so deliberately. But her very values of life made it impossible for her to see any intent in the universe, any guiding Good. All life was too accidental, too without justice, for her to bow her head in reverence. She did not see its sweep, its magnificence, its beauty, so there was nothing left.

She carried the new child grudgingly. Physically she felt miserable. There was no buoyance of spirit. On the Fourth of March, 1900, she accompanied visiting relatives to the Inaugural Parade. A camp chair on which she was standing capsized under her. The next day, symptoms of a miscarriage appeared. She walked the floor of her room, deliberating, before she sent for Dr. Hull.

"I am willing to go right ahead and keep on my feet and have the miscarriage," she told him, adding hastily, "rather than have an abnormal child."

The mild little man looked at her strangely.

"A threatened miscarriage does no harm to the child," he said.

He stroked his mousy mustache, summoned his courage before this tall lean woman who burned with a fierce determination that for a moment he half understood.

"I hope you realize, Mrs. Kinnan," he said slowly, "that a miscarriage this late in the pregnancy, or a pre-mature birth, imperils your life even more than that of the coming child. It might very well leave one—or two—children motherless."

She tapped her foot; without a word began to undress—done with Dr. Hull, hardly conscious of his presence—and went to bed and followed his instructions eagerly.

In early April "little Arthur" was safely born.

Marjorie was brought in to look at him in his bassinet. She peered over the edge of the basket, then walked indifferently away. The age of four, under her intensive training, was not too early to realize that she was the only one who mattered.

Years later her mother confided to her, "Poor Arthur—I didn't give him the chance I gave you. I didn't give him any pre-natal attention at all. Somehow, I had the feeling that he would never really be born."

Little Arthur's boyhood reflected these things as naturally as the shadow of a cloud passes over a pool. His sister ignored him or quarreled with him. He had a mania for eating the soap in the bathroom. It took the commonsense of his grandmother Traphagen when Ida took the children home for a summer visit, to say:

"Idy, don't slap that child's hands for eating that soap. The boy's hungry. I declare, you don't pay enough attention to him. You think it's so cute for that Marjorie to chew the juice out of her pieces of meat and then take them out of her mouth and put them back on the plate, with that ladified air you're teaching her, and while she's a-doing that, you aren't seeing that the boy gets the right things to eat. I'm going to look after him myself."

Little Arthur was sullen and ugly. He developed a defense mechanism of tantrums, the only way to get attention. He howled to be carried down stairs. Ida would lead him down by the hand, drag him down, and he would scramble immediately back to the top and shriek to be carried. She turned down his small breeches and spanked him soundly until he cried himself into quiet and good behavior.

Ida would say to ladies, calling on her:

"The children are so different. I could always reason with Marjorie. As a little bit of thing, I only had to explain to her why she must or must not do certain things. But Arthur doesn't know what reason is. A good spanking is the only thing that does him any good. Sometimes I think he likes to be spanked."

On the outskirts Marjorie sat smugly, listening. She walked past her brother, sniffing ostentatiously. As soon as her vocabulary was equal to it, she tormented him with adult phrases.

"You're an aggravating mortal!" she snapped.

He ran screaming to his mother.

"Mother, Mother, she called me a mortal!"

"Oh, Arthur, behave yourself. Everyone's a mortal."

"They are not," he wailed. "She just said it to be mean."

Which was true enough.

Then he would fall back on the bitter remark with which, until he was grown, he solaced himself.

"I know. You like her better'n you do me. You like her better. I know."

The other condition on which Ida had not reckoned, was the impassioned love that grew up between father and daughter. Arthur was enamored of the child. The wispy hair and the wide snub nose flecked with freckles (like a turkey's egg, he told her) that were a matter of distress to Ida, were to him further objects of adoration. On the mornings when she still slept and he could not kiss the child good-bye, he left messages. He left a verse under her breakfast plate one morning.

"I love my little daughter

From her head clear to her toes.

I even love the little bit

Of turkey-eggy nose."

Ida was disgusted. She literally suffered when he made light of the child's discrepancies. She did not want the child to make light of them too. They could all be remedied, must be. The hair could be kept religiously curled. Somewhere there was a magic freckle lotion that would really work.

She was not specifically jealous of the love between the two. It did not pain her to see the child twining her skinny little arms around his neck, smothering him with kisses, vying with him in the inventing of pet names. It made a pretty picture; and pretty pictures were most important. It did pain her to see him traducing her daughter's mind. The danger lay there. The danger of losing her, of losing control of her, of being unable to shape her to the destinies she had in mind.

She heard Arthur teaching that wealth was pleasant, if wisely used, but unimportant. Social position was a will-o'-the-wisp not worth the following. Fame was splendid, if noble and deserved. Fine raiment was folly. If one was decently and becomingly clothed, nothing more was necessary. The homage of men was a thing more dangerous in a woman's life than desirable.

Ida was in a panic that he might wean the child to "those awful Kinnan ideas". When Arthur refused to attend a reception with her one day, and went trudging off in the rain with his daughter, taking a lunch to be eaten outdoors, jealousy at last swept over her in a physical torment. For the first time the girl seemed to belong to him and not to her. If she turned out to be pure Kinnan, after all, it meant that she would be "strong-minded" and a little odd; over-intellectualized. The menace of "queerness" was ever present.

One night she awoke with a start and a certainty that Marjorie was not in her bed. Truly, the child was gone. She flew downstairs in her high-necked voluminous gown, her two long braids of hair flapping over her thin shoulders, to find all the doors locked from the inside. It savored of magic. Dry-mouthed, she called her husband.

"If she didn't go out of the doors," he said, "she went out of a window." That mode of exit would never have come to her mind.

He led the way, placid in his night-shirt, while Ida wrung her hands and moistened her lips. The child's window gave on a cherry tree. He chuckled, pointed. The child had indeed gone out by the window, and was now dancing madly in her nightgown around and around the chestnut tree beyond, the full moonlight plain on the flesh of her gay and spindly legs.

"She's doing the only sensible thing on a moonlit night like this," he remarked.

"Oh Arthur," she whimpered, "for Heaven's sake don't let her know you think it's cute. It isn't. It's just plain queer."

She went back to bed and lay there trembling. Arthur waited for the child to come in, without disturbing her Puckish gyrations.

Ida heard the two coming up the stairs together and knew from the fumbled gait that he was straining the child to his side. It was almost more than she could bear when she heard him say:

"You'll never know how much your father loves you. You're mine—blood of my blood, bone of my bone, flesh of my flesh."

She wanted to scream, "It's a lie! She's mine! Blood, bone and flesh, I made her!"

All her life Ida Kinnan drew a sharp line between public and private life. Her constant consciousness of a public audience was one of the anomalies of her nature. What was its source, in this homely woman reared on a Michigan farm? She had even named her daughter with an eye to the way the nomenclature would look in print. She rejected a middle name, saying:

"When she marries, the three names will sound better than if they are interrupted by an initial."

Arthur begged to name the child "Esther". It had to his ears a Biblical beauty.

Ida said, "People unfamiliar with your name, seeing it in print, are likely enough as it is, to accent it on the first syllable, which makes an Irish mess of it instead of good Scotch. If you call her that, it will surely be pronounced 'Esther *Kinn*-an' and not Kin-*nan*".

She already saw the name on concert programs, in society items. Arthur guffawed.

"For God's sake call her 'Victoria'," he mocked her genially.

She gave elaborate children's parties. On Marjorie's seventh birthday, a formal entertainment was staged on the ample grounds under the oak trees. There were strings of Japanese lanterns, a supper worthy of Delmonico, over which she had slaved for days. The *pièce de résistance* was a treasure tree for the little guests. A small choice fruit tree on the lawn was laden with gifts, wrapped in tissue paper and tied to the twigs with pink and blue satin ribbons. At a given signal, the company was to walk in presumed decorum to the tree and each remove a present. Pink ribbons for the boys and blue for the girls.

At the sign, the guests rushed pell-mell and ripped the specimen tree limb from limb. Lightning could not have more completely demolished it. Ribbons and scraps of paper strewed the lawn. The treasure tree was not even a success for the host-children, for in her own scramble, when she saw the rush begin, Marjorie had tripped and sprawled and lay gasping for breath, and little Arthur at this juncture became violently ill from excitement and from over-eating.

"I hope you're cured, Ida," twinkled Arthur. "The next time I think I'd entertain in the sand box."

She glared at him. What she had had in mind was the accustoming of her daughter, early in life, to the social atmosphere.

"This neighborhood is middle-class," she retorted tartly. It was the first time she had reproached him for the unfashionableness of their location. "What more could you expect of such common children?"

He was frankly puzzled.

"But my dear, we are middle-class. Why should we pretend to anything else?"

She was a Joan of Arc in a moment, buckling on her armor in her sacred cause.

"Is that any reason why a lovely little daughter should be middle-class? We aren't fit to be her parents if we can't give her anything better than what we've known."

The "something better" went on. Ida arranged for dancing lessons at a little school nearby. Starched and ruffled, the child was escorted once a week to Miss Howe's to do the splits, to kick a hat held high, to make meaningless little mincing steps. Miss Howe assured the mother that she was doing nicely, very nicely, but it was obvious even to Ida's prejudiced eye that the girl had little instinct for grace or rhythm. She mastered the simple movements only through earnest labor.

Ida was prey to all photographers. At every change of her child's expression, she rushed her to a studio and selected the most flattering pose from a mass of proofs. She admonished her never, in later life, to allow anyone to take her profile. The snub nose was hopeless.

The formality of parties, of dancing lessons, of posing, was one thing. Every-day life was another. Although she insisted on knowing where her daughter played, how and with whom, she preferred that she play away from home, or at least out of the house. Swarms of children racked her nerves with their noise. They tracked up her immaculate house. All of them seemed dirty and common to her. And the girl seemed possessed to play with Edna, who was greenish and fox-toothed and was always eating sour pickles, and with Helen Bailey, whose father drank. Marjorie thought it was great fun to hide quivering on the attic stairs with Helen when they brought Old Man Bailey home. The children were always shoo-ed out as he was brought scuffling in, snorting and blowing and sometimes singing. True, it was an awful disgrace, and she was sorry for Helen when she cried, when people said things, but it was very exciting just the same.

Sometimes when Marjorie brought a playmate home, the dust of Ida's housecleaning drove them away again. The maids of the early prosperous years were encouraged to send other children away. Twice Marjorie brought home a friend to dinner, to be met with such disapproval that she did not try it again. Ida was not "prepared" for company. It was disgraceful to have an outsider stumble in on a simple meal. Luncheon or dinner guests of any age called for desperate effort beforehand. When Ida had her Ladies' Club to luncheon, she was done up for days after.

With or without help, she tied her head up and scoured and scrubbed almost until the door-bell announced the "company". Arthur tried to break her of such absurdities by making fun of her. He tried desperate means. To quite formal guests one evening he said, as they complimented her,

"Yes, doesn't she look nice? Isn't the table pretty? Aren't things delicious? But Lord love us, you should have been here an hour ago! She had her head in a towel, and the mop was flying, the children were driven out of doors, nobody had any lunch, and she just got her pail of scrubbing water emptied as you were coming up the steps."

But he only succeeded in startling the guests, who wondered if this was one of Mr. Kinnan's famous jokes, and offended his wife past forgiving. She was incurable.

To prevent children from running in and out in her absence, Ida usually locked up the house on a trip to town. If she was delayed, Marjorie and Arthur, returning from school, played in the yard until her return, or in inclement weather, sat together in the doorway.

One winter's day Ida did not return from town, even by dinner time. Arthur was out of the city. She was combing Washington for a costume for her daughter's appearance in a school play. The house was locked. Little Arthur went to sleep on the front porch. Marjorie sat on the stone steps of the terrace. Up the street came a distinguished-looking woman, who stared at the house numbers and in a throaty voice introduced herself to the child.

She was Aunt Effie's friend—a real actress. Yes, she was playing in Washington for the week. And was Mother home? No? Then she would gladly wait for her.

The child was forced to confess that it was impossible to get into the house. The great lady graciously sat down on the steps and heard the story of the school play. Late afternoon became twilight. Lights shone out in all the other houses along the street. The gnome-like lamp-lighter pattered down the sidewalk with his stumpy ladder and his singing torch.

A chilly wind came up with the dark. The actress ran out of talk. At last she said that she would miss her evening performance if she did not leave—she was so sorry. In humiliation, the child saw her vanish into the night. If the house had been open, she could have entertained her. She could even have made tea and toast for her. Arthur awoke and fretted. Marjorie held him against her and wept bitterly.

At half-past eight Ida's lean figure came out of the darkness. Her face was twisted with a neuralgic headache. She had forgotten to eat all day. She had gone on foot to every costume shop in the city, but she bore under her arm just the correct thing.

For once, the child did not thrill to the clothes that were to glorify her. Aunt Effie's friend had been here ever since afternoon and she couldn't take her in the house. In her search of physical triumphs, it did not occur to Ida that the locked door was a bit of spiritual inadequacy that invalidated everything she was trying to do.

During the foundation years, it seemed inexplicable to Ida that the little girl was even more interested in seeing her mother in pretty clothes than in wearing them herself. The child was only too flippant about her own apparel, on the occasions when she was not properly subdued into self-consciousness.

One Easter found the Kinnan exchequer unexpectedly lean. Even Ida was willing to have Marjorie appear without the usually vital new Easter hat. She refused to buy her cheap things. The simple juvenile hats were more expensive than her own. Marjorie's spring hat of the year before had been a turned-up tricorne. Ida steamed it, turned down the wide brim, and put on a new ribbon.

On Sunday afternoon, she heard whoops of laughter on the lawn.

Marjorie was putting on a show for the other children. She had discovered that by walking in apparent demureness and giving her ears a strong twitch, she could make the done-over hat suddenly shoot up its sides to their original position.

Ida tapped on the window and called her in.

"You didn't have to give it away like that," she scolded. "If you had behaved yourself, nobody would have known it was your old hat. What will people think?"

The proper chagrin overcame the girl and she cried.

For her school clothes, she only asked not to be conspicuous. But conspicuous she was, in the strikingly simple things suitable to a millionaire child chastely costumed by De Pinna.

Ida said, "You needn't complain. I know perfectly well that you're not dressed like the other little girls. I don't intend that you shall be. Mother knows. Until you come to know people of a higher class, I intend that you shall always be dressed *better* than the other little girls. You are better, you know."

"Am I?"

"Certainly."

<hr/>

At this time, money was usually adequate enough for Ida too to dress well. Arthur's brother, Dr. William Kinnan, was now in the Patent Office too, and his socially gifted wife, Jenny, had taken Ida under the cloak of her own charm and inducted her into a small club of pleasant, well-to-do women. Ida had good tailored suits, good hats, a truly gorgeous black lace evening gown. When she was ready for a function, and Arthur, distinguished in his frock coat and silk hat, slipped his thin gold watch that his sisters Marjorie and Wilmer had all but starved to give him, into his vest pocket, and his black seal ring on his finger, Marjorie and little Arthur joined hands and danced around them in delight. Sometimes "Mr. Kinnan" was asked by his friend Ely, superintendent of schools, to make a holiday address at one of the public schools. When one year he spoke at Marjorie's own, gracious and genial, she was thrilled as never for her own small appearances. This was honor. This was joy.

They were sweet and prosperous days for Ida. She could see how, with things going as they were, she could offer a decent enough background so that the girl might have an adequate social life. Marjorie was too young to have her voice foretold, but there had been successful enough school and church plays. Sunday school had been Ida's sop to convention. Here the girl had "recited" a solemn piece to organ music in what seemed to the quivering Ida a voice of operatic timbre. She would never have believed that there were titters on the other side of the church.

Ida was happier than she had been since the days of the Fenton Ladies' Band.

There is a picture of her at this time, pretty enough to be unrecognizable. She was full of a pink silk party dress for Marjorie, and the impulse to have her own picture taken was part of her enthusiasm. There is a comb in her softly coiled hair. The face glows with a soft light, a sweet satisfaction, worthy of a better cause.

She possessed a blue mull dress, the full skirt flounced, ruffled like a billowy pale sky. One starry evening, Marjorie coaxed her into putting on the dress and walking up and down with her under the chestnut tree. The child held her fingers tight, rapt and hushed, murmuring over and over, "My beautiful mother—my beautiful mother."

She longed for beauty in her mother; Ida's awkwardness, lankness, her homeliness as she worked herself sick at cooking and housekeeping, repulsed her. She hated the artificial bosoms and the "transformations" that sprawled over Ida's dressing table like dead, tangled animals. She hated her mother's nervous frenzy over clothes, over "company", over the "impression" that she wanted the child to make on someone.

But when the woman dropped her struggles for a moment and was graciously herself, a self-respecting, well-dressed personality, the child was filled with tenderness for her.

The Farm

Arthur bought the farm almost before Ida realized what he was doing. For a year he had been talking of the desirability of land, but during that year she had been preoccupied with the change that was coming over her ten-year-old daughter.

It had been a worried twelve months. Arthur had taken his law degree and longed for escape from the Patent Office. He was a man loved of other men. There seemed no question but that in time he would succeed if he broke loose. But he had scarcely a dollar ahead. The wife who spread out his salary so patiently, the two children created by such varying desires, were chains. He waited for her to say the word that would give up his assured income and launch them on a sea of risk. Because fundamentally she mistrusted him, she did not say it. She was not ready for other worries while her handiwork was threatening to go to pieces before her eyes.

At the age of nine, it had been determined without question that Marjorie could never sing. The vocal equipment simply was not there. She had reported to her parents that she was singing with the altos at school. Her mother ordered her to request the teacher to place her with the sopranos.

"Mother doesn't want my voice to be ruined," she announced primly.

The weary schoolmistress spoke caustically.

"Please tell your mother, my dear, that you have no voice to ruin."

Ida smuggled the girl to a vocal instructor. She piped a few shrill bars. The man smiled tolerantly.

"Do not waste one cent, Madam. I do not always dare to be so positive, for adolescence, maturity, often change the whole texture of a voice. But here—no. Never."

"You might make a dancer of her," he offered helpfully. "Perhaps an actress. She will make, I believe, the Gibson girl."

Even this straw was of no use to the drowning Ida. She had watched the continued shapelessness of that pug nose too long.

The child's appearance at this age was completely distressing. She was gangling, bony. She threatened to carry on the Traphagen Jack-on-the-stick legs forever and forever. She had the high cheekbones of the Traphagen's, but a moonlike roundness of face and an unbecoming width between the eyes that were of no family. True, her mouth was not large, like Ida's, but it bore the compressed thinness of the egoist.

Her hair, after years of hot irons, was reduced to burnt strings. It was necessary to have it cut short and straight. She still bore traces of the moot freckles. Her forearms developed a coat of dark hair over which Ida agonized. Long-sleeved dresses were the order whenever possible. Ida showed her how to sit at parties, holding the inner arms up and hiding the hair. She saw to it that the girl suffered as she did. Together they shed tears and used depilatories. Years later the girl said:

"Mother, I just happened to look at my arms, and that fuzz we used to worry so about is scarcely visible. Have I out-grown it, or did we exaggerate about it when I was a child?"

Ida looked at her appealingly.

"I wanted you to be perfect," she said simply.

All in all, the girl's good points in late childhood were only her apple-cheeked health and the bubbling vitality natural to one impressed, as she was, with her own importance.

Distraught over these developments, Ida scarcely listened to Arthur's schemings for a farm. He had always talked this way. He was explaining to her now that any land outside of the nation's capital was a sound investment. He could go on with his salaried position and yet build up desirable properties against their old age. He could make a dairy-farm self-supporting. In time it would take care of them. And although he did not say so, he meant that it would also give him the contact with the soil necessary to the very preservation of his soul and sanity.

He fairly hypnotized her into agreeing with his statements. There were times when he was irresistible. She could not deny the soundness of his arguments. There was a beautiful piece of farm land ten miles out of Washington. The price was absurdly low. He would exchange their present house, the lot on which it stood and the lot on the east side, for the farm. He could mortgage the west lot and put up another house on it. It meant carrying new mortgages on the new house, starting all over again as it were, and "developing" the farm. But some day that farm would be worth $40,000, $100,000—anything. She could see that, couldn't she? Yes, that seemed plausible.

But when he came bounding home one evening with his long stride, slapping his newspaper against his leg as he walked, seized the two children and threw them in the air in turn, and exclaimed, "Well, we've got our farm!", she thought she would faint away. She went white and sat down in a kitchen chair and had to be brought a glass of water.

Retrogression. Failure. She felt as though she were on a train riding backwards. Back through years of life to the farm—

Arthur's Maryland farm was scenically beautiful and all but sterile. One length of its two hundred and forty acres lay along Rock Creek. The other boundaries were gracious woods. It sloped up and down, up and down, in curves as lovely as a Venus' body. On its charms Arthur expended the passion he had never given a woman. The low slope down from the old white farmhouse was a picturesque rocky strip ending at the foot in a cold deep spring. The largest stretch of woods, the forty-acre section, was high-vaulted and dusky as a cathedral. In its center it broke out into a miniature wild park, with hawthorn, wild plum, spicewood and paw-paw trees, and a fringe of fern and lilies along an unexpected silver brook. Arthur could not keep his secret. On this spot, when the farm was able to support them, he would build a country house and retire.

Ida threw up her hands in despair. It was not only a farm to her, but, unlike the trim prosperity of her father's acres, an abandoned farm, a haunt of desolation.

"It's folly, Arthur," she said quietly. "Utter folly."

But the harm was done. Perhaps, she thought, he would grow tired of it and sell it, before the girl was grown. She could see that it would be nothing but a drain on their resources. But she followed him bravely. Even, in what seemed to her his madness, she felt a little tenderness for him. His enthusiasm seemed to her so boyish and so pitiful.

For eight years every cent above the barest living expenses went into the building up of the farm. Its deed went back to a grant of Cavalier times. For three hundred years, produce had been taken from its un-grudging soil and nothing returned. It was worn out. Arthur pored over bulletins of the Department of Agriculture and went about preaching the gospel of the rotation of crops with a Methodist fervor. Alfalfa; turn under; corn. Alfalfa; turn under; rye. He corresponded with remote agricultural schools. He bought fertilizer by the carload. He went back and forth on the train from Brookland to Garret Park, or took the Rockville trolley in Georgetown and walked two miles in to the farm from the Rockville Pike. He had at first a series of thieving, incompetent tenant farmers, stumbling at last on Redmon. Red-headed Redmon, with his sandy mustache and his chew.

Redmon had outworn his employment in two counties. He was "the best man in the world", they said, until he got drunk. Then, every few weeks, the rain might fall on the ripe hayfields, the cows might go unmilked, the mules unwatered, for all of Redmon. He was whooping it up with his Irish gods. Perhaps it was a hangover of the persuasiveness of generations of preachers. More likely it was his own enthusiasm, in which he allowed Redmon to share. But to the gaping astonishment of past employers, Mr. Kinnan could keep Redmon sober a year at a time. Then, when he saw the storm inevitably brewing, he would say:

"Redmon, see me through the silo filling," or the harvesting, or what-ever the next work might be, "and I'll give you ten dollars extra and two weeks off."

Redmon would work industriously and even room up the stock, like a woman making all ready before her confinements. Then he would go to Rockville. On his return, days later, he would dance for hours on top of a table in the farmyard, clad in red flannel underwear.

Arthur began with a few grade cows. Gradually he replaced them with registered stock. At the end of eight years, he had a herd of nearly a hundred thorough-bred Holsteins and Guernseys, richly black and white and spotted against the Maryland meadows. He replaced the old barns with new ones; huge red structures splendid with the newest thing in stalls and stanchions. The cement foundation he laid with his own hands, hurrying out from his office, often without dinner, to use up the last shred of daylight. He piped water from the deep icy spring up the steep grade to the barns; dug his own ditches; slaved over the engine; laid his own pipe. These things could not have come about, otherwise. At last, adjoining the barns, he installed a modern dairy room, with a cooler system filled from his own cold spring water. His milk and cream went to a Washington chain of dairy lunches.

He built bricks without straw. He performed miracles, for very love of the land. There was enough money for lumber and cement and piping and engines, but not a cent left over for labor. He was architect, engineer, carpenter and Hunky. The barren soil struggled back to fertility, and corn and oats and rye and clover grew where before there had been thistles and wild dewberries.

Ida would scarcely have been more disturbed if he had been lavishing his hard-earned salary on another woman. When she first began to feel the financial pinch, she cut down on her own clothes, as a matter of course. The maid was gone. She cut corners here and there on the table. She hated living in a mortgaged house again, although the new home was prettier than the old. She mended linens that hitherto she would have discarded. Finally the time came when the grocery bill had mounted to an embarrassing figure, and Arthur was grave whenever he handed her a bill from his wallet.

Sometimes he laid his monthly salary on the table, saying:

"Fifty for Redmon. I must pay that old fertilizer bill this month, or my credit will go. A hundred. Will thirty carry this time?"

Sometimes when he laid out the money for wages, for feed, for equipment, for harvesting, for building, there was nothing left for the household. Then he would go back over it and decide which item he could leave unpaid a little longer.

The winter that he finished the barns, he had his back to the wall, fighting for time. For all her disapproval, Ida would not harass him when he was down. She had been forbearing, letting the girl go a little shabby until Spring. But on a February day, when a bitter storm caught her down-town with her daughter, she saw the girl blue-lipped and shivering in her thin coat. Ida had a thick sweater under her own light suit jacket, but that of course was different.

She came home and walked the floor, tears streaming down her face. She prepared no dinner. When her husband came in, she faced him in the doorway.

"This has gone far enough," she stormed. "You're sinking your money and our very lives in that God-forsaken Maryland farm. I hate every acre of it. Silos, cattle, you go to Pennsylvania to buy a team of mules. A new bull, a pumping system, new barns—and now your daughter hasn't clothes enough to keep warm. My wildest fears never imagined anything like this."

"How much do you need?"

She softened. She had expected the usual evasion.

"I can get her something plain for ten."

He handed her a twenty-dollar bill from his tattered bill-fold. He sank down wearily on the hall seat.

"God, Ida, I want to do the right thing. The last thing in the world I want to do is make any of you go cold or hungry or shabby."

He sprang up and took her by the shoulders.

"Give me a little longer, Ida. Just a few years more. If it goes the way I've planned, I'll have the finest dairy-farm in Maryland. It means comfort for all of us—a beautiful life, Ida. And the city is growing out that way. It won't be long before you'll see a suburban development out the Pike—"

She laughed hysterically and turned away.

From then on, he fought his battle alone. He talked to himself. He looked at his beloved daughter from a distance, with torment in his eyes. He lapsed into wistful phrases from early Methodism, saying to the girl tenderly:

"Lord love it and bless it and keep it and cause the sun to shine upon it."

His economies grew desperate. He often lunched on a handful of nuts. He startled his children at dinner one night by rapping suddenly on the table and shouting wildly,

"You children stop being so wasteful! Look at all the fruit you've left on those plum pits! Lick those plum pits!"

The children looked at each other and broke into uncontrollable giggling. The man rose from the table and went out into the night. Ida called Marjorie from her brother and confided her fears.

"Marjorie, have you noticed anything strange about your father lately? It's an awful thing to think, but sometimes I wonder if this farm business isn't making him a little insane."

The girl dismissed the matter lightly.

"Oh he's probably just worrying."

Arthur returned at midnight, gaunt, but himself.

"I'm sorry, Dide," he said and held her to him.

She patted his arm. He was only hunting beauty and peace and happiness, and she was straining away from all these things. She did not understand him, but out of her ignorance she pitied him who needed no pity.

❧

The children loved the farm. Ida excused it in the boy, for to him it was only a place to play. The girl's passion for it seemed traitorous.

The first summer of his ownership, Arthur coaxed her to camp on it for a few weeks of the children's vacation. He was so sure that none could fail to love it, who knew it. In past years he had sent his family away for the summer, to the Traphagen farm in Michigan, to the mountains of West Virginia and even, in prosperous days, to the coast of Maine. That was all out of the question now.

At first Ida refused point-blank. She would have nothing to do with the farm. The children teased her. She liked to have Marjorie coax her, pecking at her with hypocritical kisses. Even the semblance of affection from the child was a gratification. She agreed to go for two weeks.

Arthur, hilarious, set up a large tent with side walls, a board floor and a fly. He chose for site a locust grove on a hilltop overlooking the windings of Rock Creek. The rising moon put you to sleep and the rising sun awakened you.

On their first night in camp, the whippoorwills in the valley below sobbed all night in the moonlight. The wind shivered the thin locust leaves. The frogs shrilled on their silver pipes, and the deep cow bells sounded, and then were still, and tinkled again, as Peg and Laura and Bess and the gray heifer grazed and moved. At dawn Arthur wakened his daughter to hear the phoebe-bird.

"Phoe-be, where-are-you! Where-are-you! He-e-e—ere!"

All morning the locust grove and the Creek's valley were riotous with song. The Kentucky cardinal rippled his scarlet notes from sycamore to sycamore, and the meadowlark, the bob-o-link and the Maryland yellow-throat sang more chastely from the shrubbery. In the late afternoon the plover went crying across the meadow in front of the camp. Just at dusk, for it was Wednesday evening, the church bells of Kensington sounded from four miles away with an ineffable sweetness. The air was spiced with pennyroyal, with clover, with locust blossoms, wild roses and the grassy smell of the cows.

Arthur said, "Isn't it beautiful, Ida?"

And Ida said, "It's all so sad——."

But the peace of it sunk into her, in spite of herself, and she found herself glad to rest from the immaculacy of floors and curtains; glad to forget, away from her perpetual imagined audience, her grim battle in behalf of her child. There was none here to see, and she could relax, and let the girl run wild. She excused her laxness to herself by saying that the freedom was good for the health of the children. The sentry must occasionally sleep.

She stayed in camp all summer. Every year she allowed her family to coax her to the farm. She would not admit any eagerness of her own, but it was there. The camp became a matter of three canvas buildings and a netted dining room. There were cream and butter and eggs and chickens from Redmon's wife, turkeys and ducks and fresh fruits and vegetables. The children wore overalls and for baths took to the Creek.

Arthur was pathetically happy when they were all there with him. His birdlike whistle could be heard all over the farm. He usually walked the two miles to the station in the morning. At the foot of the hill, before the road went into the woods, he always stopped and waved back to his family, no matter how great his hurry. Ida, under a strange compulsion of tenderness, waved back. She did it unwillingly and felt silly.

Sometimes he had Redmon hitch up old Dan to the light buggy he had bought at a bargain, and the children drove him to the train. Ida did not go, because there were the breakfast dishes to wash. She listened with straining ears to the last click of Dan's hooves as the buggy swept into the leaf-carpeted woods. Now and again their voices would float back and up to her, deep from the cool woods. Sometimes Arthur was singing in his rich voice, and Marjorie too, in her small unlovely tones that would never have an audience.

pseudo-adult writing would have been recognized for sounding brass—the most dangerous development possible.

Ida was prepared from the beginning to combat any over-intellectualism in the girl's work. She would have been horrified at having a George Sand on her hands. She would have preferred any other path than this to glory, but she could no longer choose. Half a loaf was better than none. There was enormous prestige, plenty of money, and no doubt a distinguished marriage, in a Gene Stratton Porter or a Myrtle Reed.

"Don't try to write such queer things," Ida often said. "You are at your best in the sweet and simple things. People want to read happy things. You won't make any kind of name for yourself if you are peculiar."

The girl, even in her smugness, was groping up the side roads for beauty, as had her father. And always, Ida, alarmed, tugged at her to keep her on the main highway; to win applause with the kind of thing people wanted to read and buy; to keep her ear to the ground for the things that people might say. She could not understand why there began to be friction between herself and the girl.

Marjorie was quick to take advantage of her mother's absorption in the new talent. She wrote only under "inspiration". She soon found that the Muse was most obliging, for instance, when housecleaning was forward. Ida permitted the girl very little in the way of housework, at best.

"I don't expect you ever to have to do it—I hope and pray that you will never have to do it. I don't want you to do the things I've had to do all my life. My hands are into it—let them stay."

But such simple helps as dishwiping or the dusting of a little furniture, she asked of her. Now, if a pained expression came over Marjorie's face, at mention of these needs, Ida would say:

"What's the matter? Do you feel like writing? If you've got an inspiration, I'd rather you wrote."

And nine times out of ten, indeed yes, she had an inspiration.

After an hour's safe dawdling with pencil and paper, she would confess that somehow, it just wouldn't seem to come. So seriously, so ridiculously, so heart-rendingly seriously, did they both take the matter that both of them believed it.

Years later, the grown woman, finding it easiest to work at her cheap hack writing in the midst of household tasks crying to be done, remembered the "inspiration" and was thoughtful.

Beaus for Ida's Daughter

Ida watched anxiously for signs that boys were going to like Marjorie. She began encouragingly enough at the age of seven with Jimmy Monahan. It was impossible to approve of the Monahan family, for they were Irish, showy and quarrelsome, but Jimmy was a symbol. Whether he had a large allowance, as he claimed, or calmly pilfered it, he was always primed with sums of money up to two dollars which Ida was delighted to see him spend on her daughter. He called gravely for her in the afternoon and escorted her to Dr. Lennon's soda fountain. Out of the goodness of his heart, and with the mistaken idea that thus might he curry favor with his lady, he sometimes invited little Arthur to go along. After little Arthur had consumed three strawberry sodas at one sitting, he was no longer invited.

"All your little boy thinks about," Jimmy reported to Ida, "is his little belly."

Jimmy brought Marjorie the most sophisticated gifts of candy and flowers. He made an art of giving. He stopped short of a bottle of perfume, for little Molly Monahan, in a sisterly rage, had broken it.

Then one day, quite calmly, Marjorie dismissed her squire. Ida was delighted. It bode well for the future. Jimmy reproached Marjorie bitterly at a public gathering.

"I spent as much as two dollars on her, all in one day," he indicted, scuffling the earth with his toe.

"And I fed her little brother, too," he continued. "Always taggin' along."

Jimmy made overtures on top of the Kinnan grape arbor, where Marjorie and Arthur sat stuffing themselves, empurpled as offspring of the Bacchus. He climbed slowly up the ladder and sat down on the viny roof, a discreet distance away. Little Arthur scrambled over to him and offered him his own bunch of Concords. He sensed dimly that life had not been so pleasant since Jimmy had been absent. Jimmy laid aside the offering and stared at his boots. He was waiting for the grapes of peace. They were not forthcoming, and in a little while he climbed down the ladder and went away.

When little Arthur prattled his version of this to Ida, she was not so well pleased. Caprice was in keeping with the character of the girl she had planned; but surely it was more judicious, after dismissing attention, to accept it back again.

There were lean years as to beaus during her daughter's adolescence. The girl was not popular with the little boys. She was too self-satisfied, more interested in herself than in them, which, as every lover knows, is fatal to romance. She was stiff and self-conscious, and consequently made them feel awkward too. Besides, they liked the girls who had taffy-pulls, whose mothers said "Hello, boys," and brought them plates of cookies and left them to themselves. There was no informality in the girl, making for ease and warmth of intercourse.

Ida sensed this, and tried to make it up with more parties. But the children squirmed and respected the girl without liking her. Ida reproached her subtly during the periods of boy-lack.

"I saw Ralph walking home from school with Miriam today. Who walked home with you?"

"I walked home by myself. I don't like Ralph anyway."

Ida arched her eyebrows coyly.

"You know, you must like them if you expect them to like you. It doesn't do a girl any harm to smile at the boys, if she does it in a ladylike way, of course."

The difference between a ladylike and an unladylike smile for the boys was beyond the girl, but urged on by the necessity for her mother's approval, she smiled. Ida was caustic when the girl fell down on her job. She was lavish with praise when she did well. The girl trotted home like a retriever dog with every scrap of a compliment given her. Ida devoured them greedily, sweet sops to her hope.

Now and then Ida was startled to see the child working to make up to some particular lad. At the age of eleven, Marjorie reported one day:

"Well, I got Merle for my beau."

"Marjorie, what on earth do you mean?"

"Well, he was going with Lottie Pace, so I just played with her all the time. Yesterday I was skating up and down around the Baptist Church and Merle was skating too. And he skated up and down past me, and finally he said, 'I noticed you're at Lottie's all the time when I'm there.' I didn't say anything and he said 'What would you say if I was to ask you to be my girl?' And then he skated away like everything, and when he skated back again, I said 'I guess I'd say all right.' So we skated up and down together with our hands crossed, and this morning when I got to school he came out to the cloakroom in front of everybody and took off my rubbers for me."

Ida was horrified. Merle, it happened, was the scum of the earth, destined, to the discerning adult eye, for degeneracy; a hunched little fellow with squinting eyes and a flat nose.

"But why Merle? I've seen a dozen boys I'd rather see come home from school with you."

"Everybody'd rather have Merle for their beau than anybody else."

"But haven't I told you that you are better than most of these children? Because Merle is good enough for Edna and Helen and May, doesn't mean he's good enough for you to play with."

The girl shrugged her shoulders impudently.

"Marjorie, I do not understand you. Sometimes I feel that I can't depend on you at all."

The proper balance between enough beaus, the right beaus—and too many beaus or the wrong beaus, gave Ida many sleepless nights. The girl must learn to "attract" men, but the bogey-man of "girls going wrong" lurked in every bush. Ida would have been outraged with any psychologist who might have told her that the attraction she so emphasized was basically sexual, and that she was playing up all the elements of sex. Men must flock around the girl of her schemes like moths to a light, but the girl must be aloof. Chastity was the candle on the altar of a woman's life.

Later, in confiding intimate details of her own life to her daughter, as she loved to do, Ida boasted "I was never a low, passionate woman."

She did not see that a woman without passion is a fire without comfort, bread without salt:

The women's magazines were full of "Tell Your Daughter!" propaganda. Mothers wrote to the *Ladies' Home Journal*:

"I neglected my little daughter. I was a coward, and did not tell her the facts of life. At the age of thirteen—thirteen, mind you!—my little girl went wrong. She passed out of our lives, and her father and I sit sorrowing alone."

It was accepted that of course a thirteen-year-old girl who had become a mother would pass out of her parents' lives. The fault might be theirs, they would admit it in print. But once the disgrace had occurred, she would have to take her infant, if it survived, and move on. She was the untouchable of the late Victorian era.

Ida so worked on her husband's emotions that he said solemnly to his daughter, "There's one thing in the world that must never happen to you. I'd rather see you dead in your coffin (the standard phrase) than see it happen. No, I can't tell you. You must ask your mother."

Ida said slyly, "You know, Marjorie, if you ever went wrong, I believe I'd stand behind you further than your father would. Much as he loves you, I feel sure he would turn you out of the door."

She felt it an opportune time to link the girl more closely to herself, to make her feel that her mother, always, was behind her. She did not have the faintest fear that her child would disgrace her.

The whole thing was Greek to the girl, as it must have been to all the girls of her generation, for whose benefit was written "What a Young Girl Should Know", and to whom were smuggled "the facts of life" like a dirty picture book. The only clear idea she could get of the situation, was that having a baby was the most awful thing that could possibly happen to a girl or woman. People got married when a girl was going to have a baby, and that made it all right. Olive Brewer had a baby when she was in the sixth grade.

Brookland hummed with it. Her own mother hadn't known there was anything the matter with her until just before it was born. A venerable judge granted special permission for Olive to marry the fourteen-year-old boy who was the father.

"I never grant children a license to marry, under any conditions," he announced profoundly, "but the extreme youth of these parents of an illegitimate child makes the circumstances so shocking, so extremely shocking, that I shall allow them to marry."

He had been reading the *Ladies' Home Journal*, too. He was roundly applauded for his generosity. Olive was married, and went on producing now legitimate offspring; puny things that lived for a few years and expired.

It was all very mysterious and terrible.

Marjorie heard Ida say, "I can't imagine why Rose Sherwin married that Post fellow," and contributed archly from her corner, feeling very wise and clever, "Ah, maybe she had to!"

Ida started. "Where did that child get such a notion!" Then she queried shrewdly, "Marjorie, you don't know anything, do you? You haven't heard anything? You must tell Mother everything, you know."

It would seem that the pure of heart can be low of mind.

The oldest boy of farmer Redmon was a pleasant red-haired yokel, who tolerated the nuisance of the two Kinnan children on the farm with a kind patience. He was hauling sand one summer for cement for Mr. Kinnan's barn foundations. He drove far up Rock Creek with his wagon, loaded it from a bed of cleanest white sand. Often he allowed his employer's children to accompany him, although they were a bother. They disappeared up the creek, wading and fishing, just as he was ready to start home. One day as he started off for a load, Marjorie ran after him and climbed on the wagon alone. He had to go further up the Creek this time for sand, and they were gone a long time. He entertained his company with tales of his own school days; yokel incidents that were his only conversational material.

"The girls' outhouse was on one side of the fence," he related, "and the boys' outhouse on the other, and we sure did torment them girls a-throwin' things over the fence when we knowed they was in there. We throwed sycamore balls and little weentsy mud cakes, nothin' to hurt nobody. But the girls sure screamed and fussed, until one day they tattled on us and the teacher done give all us boys the wust hidin' all around. And then we quit."

When the load of sand creaked into the farmhouse gates, Mrs. Redmon stood with her arms akimbo.

"You Rafe, git on down to the barn with that quick. Marjorie, you git on home to your mother. You'll find out a thing or two."

Marjorie climbed over the pasture bars and ran madly across the meadow to the locust grove. Her heart was pounding. She had a premonition of something awful. Maybe her mother was dying, while she was gone. Maybe she should have waited for little Arthur. He might have tried to follow the wagon and gotten drowned or caught in the barbed wire. Ida met her at the stile in the fence around the camp. Her long crooked nose was white with rage, the nostrils distended. Her shapeless lips were compressed to a rigid line. Her eyes were narrowed to mere slits. She lifted a long bony finger like an accusing fate and pointed it at her daughter.

"Shame!" she sneered, drawing out the vowel like a venomous snake. "Sha-a-me! A great big girl like you! Thirteen years old! Aren't you asha-a-med!"

A sense of guilt swept over the girl. Of course it was "dirty" for Rafe to talk about the outhouse. She flushed. Ida drew close and peered into her face.

"Tell me! Did anything happen?"

"I don't know what you mean, Mother."

"Did anything happen? Did you or Rafe do anything you shouldn't do?"

She shook her head. It had been necessary for her to go into the bushes while Rafe was loading sand, but she had gone way off and he couldn't have seen her. He told her about the boys throwing things at the girls in the outhouse—

"Oh indeed!" Ida's favorite disciplinary method was a sneering sarcasm, "Indeed, miss! And what else did he talk about?"

"Just about the teachers, what they looked like and how cross they were."

"And what else?"

"And about the Rockville Fair."

"Are you sure that's all?"

"Yes, Mother."

The girl was in exquisite torment. She felt unclean and sick at her stomach.

"All right. But don't let this happen again."

The girl sat on the stoop of the sleeping tent and sobbed. Ida passed back and forth, ignoring her. Finally she threw at her:

"Oh, I guess you're innocent, all right."

Every now and then, in the next few days, she would suddenly point her finger at the girl and shake her head and say "Sha-a-me!"

It was thoroughly impressed on the girl that it was dirty to be alone in the woods with a boy, especially when you were thirteen.

Ida's purpose was served. Privately, she was sure that her daughter was "pure-minded", but she could take no risks. The chastity of a Vestal Virgin must be preserved at all costs. Those destined for the temple of fame must reach there in perfect condition. She felt herself justified in the most extreme measures to make her daughter "perfect". When the girl, from now on, lashed out at her at times with every sign of hate, she attributed it to the dangerous age through which Marjorie was passing, and redoubled her vigilance.

After the Rafe episode, she screwed up her courage to give the girl "the facts of life".

"What would you think of a girl or woman who would let a man—" and she trailed off into the vaguest but most shocking details.

Marjorie wept for hours. She clung to her mother in her shock and distress.

"Oh Mother, I had no idea it was anything like that. Isn't it awful!"
Ida crawled with maternal tenderness and gratification.

"Yes, darling, it is awful. If I'd known you would be so upset, I don't think I would have told you. I thought you knew more than you did."

She could rest on her oars for a time. The girl's safety, at least, was assured.

The Battle Begins

When Marjorie was ready for high school, Ida knew that she must make a move. Brookland had been getting shabbier and shabbier. Mr. Kinnan, even as president of the Citizens' Association, would be unable much longer to keep out stores from the corner lot next to their home. The way must now be prepared in earnest for the girl's future. Brookland was no place for a battle ground. The farm was draining them dry, but she would manage somehow.

She was sorely tempted by the offer of their good friend Mrs. Holton, owner of an exclusive girls' school, to prepare the girl for college, gratis. Mrs. Holton felt that an earnest student would be most desirable in the midst of her wealthy, indifferent protégées. In contrast to their mental leisureliness, Marjorie's mind seemed to her a delight. The Holton's had been neighbors of the Kinnan's before the school was established. It was obvious even to the young girl that Mrs. Holton was the sort of woman her father should have married. It was impossible to bore her with details of the farm; she wanted one herself. She laughed boisterously with him in a camaraderie that seemed a trifle rough to the prim Ida. Her undoubted affection for the father may have increased her interest in the daughter.

Ida and Arthur talked long and solemnly over her offer. Arthur insisted from the beginning that it would be a mistake to turn their daughter loose among girls of a social and moneyed standing so far above her own as to make contact a torture and not a benefit. He was thinking of the happiness of the child herself. To Ida it seemed, at first, that the opportunity was priceless. But at last she came to see that Marjorie would surely suffer the embarrassment of the charity student; that her home background would not permit her to mingle on terms of equality; that nothing would be gained. It was too early, she decided, to throw her with the elite. Wait a few years more. If Arthur sold the farm, perhaps, when the girl was ready for college—.

Conveniently, at this moment, Ida was threatened with a nervous breakdown. She had so fretted over the coming period that she was in ragged shape. She couldn't go on with the big house any longer. It was wearing her out. The doctor told Mr. Kinnan very gravely that it was wearing her out. Very well.

Arthur sold the house and took the proceeds from his small equity to settle some farm bills. Since he had been carrying the new home and the farm too, he had done little more than pay his mortgage interest.

"You seem to have something up your sleeve, Ida," he said. "When we vacate the house, make any living arrangements you want to, that I can carry. I wash my hands of it."

Ida had thought out her plans carefully. As long as she could not afford a private school, the thing to do was to send the girl to the high school in the northwest section that drew from the better classes. Its roster bore the names of the sons and daughters of congressmen and senators, bankers and diplomats. They would take an apartment near the school. She had already, it appeared, seen a charming apartment at Thirtieth and Q, at a rent they could afford. It did not matter to Arthur when or where he went. He lived, breathed and had his being on the Maryland acres.

The apartment seemed to Ida a miracle place. The building had a

Spanish dignity, with a fountain in the court. There was a negro janitor who made watery ice cream that he sent up the dumb waiter, on order. Ida thought how dressy it would seem, almost like a hotel, to ring William for refreshments when Marjorie had unexpected callers. The apartment was not entirely modern, and the sleeping arrangements were highly congested, but the few rooms had a deceiving air of "class". The atmosphere for the most part was impeccable. The apartments were thickly populated with elderly widows, among them the spouse of an ex-commissioner of Patents. Gentility overhung the green-carpeted stairs.

Until, that is, Mrs. Nolan began to sing. Mrs. Nolan was fortunately rather tucked away in the back apartment adjoining the Kinnan's on the top floor. She was an inexplicable character, at least to the naive. She wore velvet dresses even in the morning, and ermine and orange birds of Paradise on the street. Bill collectors were forever pounding on her door, and getting no response, ringing the wheezing bell at the Kinnan's. She sang, raucously and joyously, to her own accompaniment, and kept a large aviary in the kitchen. Among the birds was a parrot with a voice as strident as her own. When she sang too long, he shrieked, "Oh Hell, oh Hell!" Mr. Nolan was away a great deal. One morning Ida asked Marjorie if she heard anything in the Nolan apartment in the night. The wall adjoined the girl's bedroom. Ida was sure she had heard a man's voice, and a man's footsteps going down the stairs at three in the morning. Mr. Nolan was in Oklahoma. But Ida, incongruously, liked the woman and did not press the point. Mrs. Nolan had said in her hoarse voice,

"Ah, Mrs. Kinnan, you're a wonderful mother. That child is going to have a future."

Ida was helplessly then her friend.

Mrs. Nolan continued, "Mr. Nolan would just love for me to have a child, but I tell him no, he's too old and fat and drinks too much. I tell you 'You change my drake and I'll show you what I can do.'"

Mrs. Kinnan, to her daughter's astonishment, was not offended. Every now and then she struck up an understanding with a Mrs. Nolan. They liked to come to her with their tales. She was a sexless oracle who often gave them the most helpful advice. Marjorie realized that her mother was lenient of any woman's shortcomings, save hers.

The day that enrollment opened for high school, Ida accompanied the girl as far as a vacant lot nearby. She would wait there for her, she said.

"Oh, Mother," reproved the daughter, "you act as if you were the one just starting to high school."

"I am—I am." Her voice broke.

"Why, that's silly—. It's silly for you to wait for me." Ida shook her head and sat down on an outcropping of stone. She handed the girl a dollar.

"If it takes a long time, and they seem to go to lunch any place, perhaps at the school, you go right along. Some real nice high school girl may speak to you."

When the girl rejoined her mother an hour or two later, she saw the woman hiding something in the bushes on her approach. She pounced on it suspiciously. It was a little parcel of soda crackers Ida had brought along for herself.

A "real nice high school girl" had indeed spoken to her. A tall, distinguished looking girl, a little older, had turned to her graciously.

"I see we're going to be in the same class. We might as well get acquainted. My name's Katherine Lyons. What is yours?"

Overcome with the materializing of her mother's prophecy, impressed as she was with its possible consequences, she had lost herself, as she was often to do, in a wave of confusion. She had stammered,

"My name's Kinnan."

It was not a propitious beginning. Ida reproached her bitterly for such plebeian awkwardness. It made a vicious circle. The next time a strange student approached her, it was even more difficult to keep her poise and answer "like a lady".

The girl's first two years were a complete social failure. The school parties came and went without her. At first she told her mother of them, but after finding Ida sitting in the kitchen on the night of one affair with the tears streaming down her face, she stopped informing her of the functions to which she was not invited. Neither she nor Ida was wise enough to know that she was simply trying too hard. As in early childhood, her stiff self-consciousness drove away more normal youth.

With something of her mother's stoicism, she plunged into her studies and into writing for the school magazine. Here she was on firmer ground. Just as Ida had begun once more to despair, she found that the girl was making a name for herself with her writings. Ida begrudged the fact that her hold on glory seemed destined to have an intellectual savour, but again, half a loaf was better than none. If the girl could achieve eminence only with her wordy little pen, so be it. But eminence there must be.

Having steeled herself to doing without the society Ida craved for her, Marjorie found its blessings were being offered her, now that she could get along comfortably without it. She was a somebody again. There were invitations to everything. There were two or three acceptable enough beaus. She was one of four asked to join a sorority.

Ida browbeat Arthur into postponing the purchase of a plow and giving her money for Marjorie's initiation dues and jeweled pin.

The band was playing down the avenue again. Ida swung into step and was off to the war with her gun on her shoulder. The light of battle was in her eyes. She was happy once more and fought off the hungry maw of the farm to pay for dressmakers and silk party dresses. She and the girl were intimate again, reveling in petty triumphs. Marjorie dropped back comfortably into the arms of approval and lapped up her mother's absorption like warm cream.

A wise old general by this time, Ida made a flank attack. If Arthur would let the girl go to dancing school this winter, she would sublet the apartment a month earlier in the summer and for a month later in the fall. That meant two more months of comfortable living on the farm for him. He fell into the trap. The school Ida signed up for was one of the most expensive in the city.

Aside from its tuition, there were satin dancing slippers, silk stockings, party dresses, and even, on wet or stormy nights, the expense of a hack. Ida put the girl on the trolley and met the one that brought her back, waiting humbly in the shadows like any serving woman. She drank in all the details of the evenings. Senator so-and-so's son had joined the class. One of the girls had invited the nephew of the president to the Spring German. She must show her mother the steps she had learned. Had anyone spoken of her new dress? Ida lived more and more vicariously.

The high spot of the year for her was when her daughter began receiving a weekly and anonymous box of flowers. Each Tuesday the square white container was delivered, to reveal each time a corsage bouquet more exquisite than the last. Violets clustered around a red rose. Lilies of the valley dripping through sweet peas most startlingly out of season. Freesias and yellow rosebuds. Tiny sweetheart roses. One great brown orchid. Nothing could have been more unsuitable on the flat breast of a sixteen-year-old girl, but Ida encouraged her to wear them to school, for all the world to see. Ida palpitated over the possibilities of the situation. She indulged dreams she had kept smothered for sixteen years. Some youth of unlimited means was adoring from a distance. Of course, she wouldn't want the girl to marry too early, but if the right young man came along, it would be folly to interfere with the match. He probably drove a car and went to Europe in the summer. When the truth came out, at the end of the year, Ida was crushed. After a moment's dismay, Marjorie burst into laughter. "Just like your father," Ida lamented.

The flowers had been tribute from the morbid "crush" of another girl, who had walked to school and saved her lunch money to buy them.

The dancing school produced no startling results. The friendship of Harry was its only lasting consequence. Harry was a great comfort to Ida. As long as her daughter could fall back on the devotion of a Harry, all was well. If his family had been less of the world, less comfortably "fixed", she would not have approved of him at all. If they had been more so, she would have found him everything desirable. As it was, she withheld judgment, awaiting developments. Marjorie was plainly not growing any undue affection for him. It was a little early to be disturbed about anything—.

Harry invited Marjorie to go to the dancing school's spring cotillion with him. He and his mother called for her in their carriage. Mrs. B— dutifully mounted the three flights of stairs to call on the girl's mother. Mrs. B— was very much the lady, very gorgeously gowned. Their money was hotel money, which to Ida was not quite respectable. It reminded her of Jay Conrad—.

Little Arthur stalked back and forth through the hall, scowling at everybody. Marjorie ran through, gathering up last-minute handker-chief and slipper bag. He jostled her.

"M-yah! Think you're smart. All dressed up!"

She brushed past him insolently. He was starved for attention.

Ida entertained her caller in stiff embarrassment. She was "caught", as she phrased it. Her one thought all day had been the girl's preparation. She had taken her to a hairdresser in the morning and had supervised an elaborate arrangement of curls that somehow failed of the effect she had visualized. Her own hair straggled about her ears, her skirt showed spots where she had knelt, taking a last minute tuck in the party petticoat. She smoothed her hair back and ran her hand over her face nervously. Why hadn't Mrs. B— been content to meet the girl at the party and leave her alone? She could have met her when she was dressed for it, some other time. The thought of Mrs. B— as a possible pleasant friend for herself did not enter her head. She no longer troubled to make friends. She had passed imperceptibly over the border line dividing her life from her daughter's. She was now the vine clinging to the tree, drawing its sustenance from it.

Mrs. B—, to her annoyance, continued to try to draw her into the fringes of the boy and girl friendship. Mrs. B— welcomed the girl to her heart, for Harry's taste in girls had heretofore been a trifle exotic. She seemed to the girl the loveliest sort of mother to have: exquisite in appearance, gracious and entirely free of feverishness. To Ida, the recommendation of the B— household was its means and its sophistication. The neat closed carriage, the butler, the cook, the little personal maid, made up quite the proper atmosphere. Ida's daughter welcomed the calm of the house, the ease of life and of thought. The B—'s approved of her as she was, without a hectic expectation of more of her, and more and more. She came to love, not the son, but the mother. She spent easeful days and week-ends with her. Mrs. B— took the boy and girl to the theatre, and afterward to the old Raleigh Roof Garden, where the children were allowed to have lobster and beer and the orchestra director asked the young lady if she cared for any special waltz to dance by. On New Year's Eve, there was the worldliest of celebrations after the theatre, with a squab and the first champagne, and Mary Pickford and David Belasco at the next table; not quite so glamorously as today, for the taffy-curled Mary was only making a stage debut in "The Good Little Devil".

Ida sat at midnight by a window in the dark of the apartment leaning her tired head against the pane. The maple outside swished its boughs back and forth on the glass, with caressing fingers. Her daughter seldom caressed her now. The demonstrativeness of childhood was gone. Ida did not understand it, but her work was showing boomerang tendencies. The girl was fast becoming so impressed with her own potentialities that she trod roughly on the lady-in-waiting who had whispered of them in her ear. Rare moments of old Michigan common sense assailed Ida, in which it came over her that what the girl needed was not the urge to glory, but to be thrashed within an inch of her life before it was too late, and sent on her way with a normal outlook. But she could not relinquish her dreams. And some new small achievement by the girl kept her hopes warm.

She could picture the lively hotel scene tonight. The palms, the flowers, the crystal chandeliers, the scurrying waiters, the whining music. In the midst of it, dancing with Harry in his boy's dress suit, her daughter, a part of the gay, cosmopolitan life of the nation's capital. The blue chiffon dress was a success. The three-dollar material might have made up just as prettily. She had chosen this really because it was four. Yards and yards of it. Silver trimming at twelve dollars a yard. She was almost satisfied with the way the girl had looked. If her hair only stayed in curl—. The fly in the ointment was the fact that she would not hear the story of the evening until the next day, for Marjorie was spending the night with the B—'s. She always sat up, thinking, until her daughter came home. Then she got everything while the girl was fresh and vivacious and full of it all. She had noticed that sometimes the next day the girl was sullen and told her very little. That was torture.

She suffered torments of jealousy in any case over the girl's affection for the other woman. The compensation lay in Marjorie's bringing her minute descriptions of everything she had done and seen. Mrs. B—— had let Marjorie wear two of her diamond and emerald rings when they went to the roof garden; one of her simpler necklaces; had given her a filmy shawl. Yes, she could visualize the girl wearing the diamonds and emeralds——.

Mrs. B—— had insisted on Ida's accompanying their party to the Raleigh Roof one night. She had bought a new lining for the old black lace, and had her nails manicured. She didn't want to go, she didn't want to go! She smiled and nodded like an animated wax figure, to Mrs. B——'s small talk, but was almost tonguetied herself. After a glass of beer, she sat staring straight ahead of her, almost literally paralyzed. The evening had been an agony for everyone.

Marjorie had stormed.

"Couldn't you talk? Couldn't find *anything* to say?"

Ida had shaken her head dumbly.

"I just couldn't——"

Marjorie had reported Mrs. B—— as saying kindly, "I'm afraid Mother doesn't quite approve of us. Perhaps she thinks you're too young to have liquor with us. Be sure she understands that I only let you have a little."

No, Ida took no exception to the liquor. Brought up in her strict Michigan schooling—Abram had once stalked lankly into a Fenton saloon and knocked the proprietor senseless for selling young Dell a drink—she did not approve of it, in the abstract. But served with such grace and sophistication, it became something else; a mere gesture of cosmopolitanism.

A storm was brewing. The maple beat violently on the windowpane. The last light in the apartment house flicked out. A crowd of revelers clattered down the street, tooting horns and hurrying to make the owl car. A few drops of rain spotted the windowsill.

Her husband and her son were sleeping soundly. She must take the boy to the dentist soon. She had let it go too long. Arthur was snoring. He snored a good deal lately and tossed in his sleep and often awakened with a blinding headache. He didn't seem quite himself. He was pinching her allowance more and more, and he talked wildly of "just a little longer, Ida."

She couldn't sleep. The imagined music of the hotel orchestra was throbbing in her ears. Old outworn music of her day. "The Little Brown Jug". "Bring Back My Bonnie To Me". She knew they couldn't be playing those pieces, but it was all she could imagine. She remembered what deep notes she blew out of her tuba in "The Little Brown Jug" when the Fenton Ladies' Band played it. She was wide awake. No point in crawling in beside her husband and lying there all night with her eyes straining into the darkness.

She went into the kitchen and turned on a light and made herself a sandwich and finished the week's ironing.

The fourth year in the respectable apartment house brought joy and distress in mixed proportions. Little Arthur had suddenly become more amenable since his two minor operations. Ida could only think that he must have needed them very badly, but the change in him went deeper than that. She had always shown gentleness in the presence of illness that was enormously comforting. When she laid her fingers on the boy's hot forehead, and held his knobby boy hands in hers, he was suffused with gratitude and tenderness. She brought delicacies to the hospital for him and he thanked her touchingly. As he began to emerge from the ether, the nurse heard him murmuring. She leaned close. He was apolo-

recapture the tenderness he had once felt for the girl he had married, the thin, clean Michigan girl without a sense of humor.

"I haven't done enough for you, Ida," he apologized. "I should have taken you places and brought you candy, shouldn't I? I never gave you the things you wanted. They only seemed funny to me. But I'll have things in shape pretty soon, and you can have the best hat in the city of Washington. And don't take the children so seriously. You're making a slave of yourself for that girl. Don't ever let me hear her speak to you like that again."

But the situation called for drastic measures.

A few days later friction arose between mother and daughter. Nerves stretched taut. At last the girl stamped her foot and screamed,

"Oh, I hate you, I hate you!"

Ida gathered the shreds of her individuality together. She said with dignity, "Very well, if you have no feeling for me, I don't need to feel obligated to any further sacrifices for you. At your next dancing class, you may tell Mrs. Dyer that you will not attend again this winter."

"Mother! Not even the Christmas Cotillion?"

"Nothing further this winter." She walked from the room.

Then she shut herself in the bathroom until she could calm the trembling of her knees and the parched dryness of her mouth. Her daughter beat on the door, frantic with unbelief.

"Mother! I didn't mean it! You know I didn't mean it! I love you, Mother! Mother, I can't stop like that. What can I tell everybody?"

Ida sat shaking on the clothes hamper. She wanted to believe the lying voice outside. She wanted the girl to lay her smooth young cheek against her wrinkles, even if it was only to be allowed to go to dancing school again. It would be easy to believe that the girl had spoken only in a childish temper. But she knew that she was lost forever if she gave in now. No more authority; no more influence; the girl would snap her fingers at her and go her own way. Her queer way, far from the paths of glory. And it was for the girl's own good to take a little of the conceit out of her. The pendulum had swung too far. Ida could endure the slight to herself, could forget it overnight. But her daughter was losing all charm in her growing insolence. Ida held firm, and a chastened, respectful adolescent spent her Friday evenings at home.

Ida's other cause of distress was her husband's growing strangeness. The headaches were more frequent. The fashionable doctor that Ida took great consolation out of patronizing could find nothing wrong. He would awaken in the morning, blind with pain, unable to go to the office. He would take Doctor Bowman's sedative medicine, sleep a little, then come out to the kitchen where Ida was working and walk up and down in his pajamas, talking wildly of his plans. Ida told him that he was working himself into insanity.

"Honestly, Arthur, I think you're a little crazy."

One morning he slept until noon. She became alarmed and shook him.

He opened drugged eyes a moment and sank back into his deep-breathing oblivion. She telephoned the fashionable doctor from the booth in the basement. Let him sleep. It would do him good. If she insisted, he would come over later in the day. Yes, she was alarmed. His eyes had been so strange. Very well.

The janitor followed her to the foot of the stairs. Please, would she speak to the young lady? She had 'phone calls—he was glad to call any of the tenants, but she talked almost an hour, and other people complained. Yes, she would speak to her about it.

The young lady was having a new caller that night, the most adult of her experience. A young banker. Did Mother think Father was really sick? Oh no, he couldn't be. He was never sick. Ought she do anything so serious as tell the young banker not to come? Ida hesitated.

The look in his eyes when she shook him—

The nice young banker—

No, it would probably be all right. What dress was she going to put on?

Afternoon dragged on and the doctor did not come. The girl was sent to telephone again. Yes, the doctor was on his way. Ida walked back and forth between Arthur's bedroom and the room where her daughter primped for the evening.

"Marjorie, do you suppose you could boil some eggs for your brother's supper? I can't seem to think—"

Impatiently, the girl threw together a little food on the edge of the kitchen table and piled the dishes in the sink. Ida did not eat. It was time to turn on the lights for the evening. Ida lit a candle to put beside her husband's bed. The glaring overhead light was so incongruous on that strange face. He breathed in terrific rumbles. Marjorie preened in front of a mirror and tried things in her hair. Ida followed her around helplessly.

"If it wasn't so late—. I don't suppose you could reach that young man now—."

The young man arrived, ceremonious and inclined to be quite interested in Miss Kinnan. She sat facing him in a chair from which she could look over his head at the hall beyond, and still further the closed door from behind which came the annoyance of her father's snoring. Ida walked about in the hall, into the kitchen, back again; sat down on the hall seat where she could look in at her daughter, "entertaining" her caller.

The door bell jangled. The doctor's assistant had come. One of the doctor's most important clients was being confined, and they had all been most upset. Ida led him behind the closed door.

He took one startled look at the sick man, ordered all the bedding in the house piled on him, hot water bottles, heat of any sort, heat.

"Why didn't you let us know earlier? Why didn't you let us know the seriousness—"

She gathered her forces against him.

"I did let you know. Why didn't you come?"

He deflated himself. He would send his superior at once.

"Doctor, is it hopeless?"

He murmured vague terms, "acute uremic coma", donned his magnificent brown velour overcoat, and got out in confusion, mopping his forehead.

Ida eased herself to the hall seat. Why didn't the girl come out? There she sat, smirking and chatting, playing up to the young banker with a forced archness. Ida heard her say affectedly, "I should just despise to be a minister's daughter—"

Ida called to her, when she could make her voice sound above a dry whisper. The girl frowned and came out.

Ida clutched at her arm for support.

"Marjorie—oh, you're hard, you're hard! I thought your father meant more to you than that—sitting there—"

"Mother, hush! What can I do? Shall I tell him to go home?"

"No, no—we might need to send him for someone—just don't leave me. I can't stand it out here alone. I go in and look at him, and I can't stand that."

"But Mother, it can't be serious—"

"No, no, of course not—Marjorie, don't go—"

"But we can't stay out here, whispering. What will he think?"

It was the sacred rally cry.

"You come in and talk with us."

Ida followed her daughter back to the living room. She clutched the arm of her chair to hide her trembling. She moistened her lips, so that she might now and then ask a civil question. Then she stalked out of the room like a sleepwalker and behind the closed door.

"Marjorie!"

She called out in a whimpering gasp like a trapped animal. The girl had never heard so desperate a sound. She forgot the niceties of entertaining a young man and ran out.

"Your father is dying."

"How do you know? The doctor didn't say so."

But knowledge of death was in the air. The woman knew it. The young man and the girl felt their flesh creep. Only little Arthur slept on, full of the fatigue of his thirteen years, on his couch in the other bedroom, and did not hear the great wings beat suffocatingly through the middle class apartment.

The girl took charge. She had noticed that a new doctor had moved in across the street recently. Mr. Hunter, please go over and have him come immediately. She forced water down her mother's throat, pushed her into a chair and went to the basement telephone to call Doctor Bowman. Yes, Mr. Kinnan was dying. She had called another physician, but Doctor Bowman had better come.

The young banker, perspiring, followed the new doctor to the door. Hadn't he better go, or could he do something. No, wait a few minutes. He might be needed.

The new doctor was in time to go through the conscientious, futile, last-minute activity of the medical profession, with a great business of hypodermics and little vials. He arranged the body neatly, put clean sheets on the bed and lit a lamp for the bedside table. His mother had been Irish.

As he went out, he met the family physician coming in. Ida had so enjoyed saying, "Yes, Doctor Bowman of Connecticut Court is our family physician". The men nodded. The new doctor spread his hands in a gesture of helplessness.

"This man has been under your care?" he queried stiffly.

"Yes, yes. My assistant gives me shocking information of acute uremia. There had not been a symptom—"

"No? Perhaps my medical experience is not as varied as yours, but I have never known the thing to be quite so unexpected. Good evening."

Ida wavered toward Doctor Bowman.

"Doctor, what did he mean? Could he have been saved?"

"My dear woman, he only meant that this dreadful thing came out of a clear sky. Neither God nor man could have saved him," he said reverently. He sat on the golden oak hall seat and patted the widow's hands, talking beautifully of "these things in life" with the sweet lushness that made him so beloved of his patients. Everyone said that it made you feel better just to have him sit by the bed. He got away as soon as he could. The size of his bill was a sure indication that he had done everything he could. Ida and Marjorie agreed that he would never have dared send a bill like that if he had any sense of remissness.

The new doctor sent a bill for "One night call—$5.00" and told Mrs. Kinnan when he met her on the street, that she had better take care of herself or she would follow her husband.

Now, the doctors gone, the evening's caller gone, (the nice young man hurled headlong into these deep waters) the great beating wings gone grandly on, Ida could only stare dumbly at her daughter and rub her cold hands over her own dry blue lips.

The door bell whirred. The girl answered it. Will and Jenny. Arthur's brother Will, with his face twisted into a white torment. The girl drew chairs for them; began to recite the details.

Ida's eyes were riveted on her like a half-wit. She so lived in this alien creature, that now under this catastrophe, she could have no existence apart from her. Her own body did not exist, save as a numb thing she dragged about with her. She could not speak. She could only move her lips without sound. This other self was speaking for her, telling them when they sent for the doctor. What he had said—

"Isn't she calm—" her voice was no more than a hoarse titillation. "Isn't she wonderful. Jenny, she hasn't lost poise—wonderful poise—"

"Yes, Ida," pityingly. "Ida, can't you lie down? You're in dreadful shape. You must keep up, for the sake of the children."

Ida nodded and tried to swallow away the dry thing in her throat that was paralyzing her, and kept her eyes on her daughter.

Business of wiring for the relatives. The crow-like gathering of the clan. Arthur's family was together under one roof for the first time since his father's death nearly forty years before. His sisters mourned him as they would mourn a lover. Ida, seeing the inconsolability of their grief, knew with something of a pang that she had never known the meaning of love. Only her love of her child, her other self. The maternal instinct—love of oneself, extended—

Business of services in the undertaking parlors. The customary laudatory obituary, given a little more space in the papers because the deceased was a respected government official. The half dozen or so young men who, to Ida's astonishment, came around, shabby hats in hand, to add their tribute. He had given them help in attending school; found them work and given them money and even clothes. He had helped her own brothers, taking the suits off his own back to send them. The earnest young men accounted for some of the occasions when Arthur had refused her money for Marjorie's clothes; occasions when she was sure the farm did not need it all.

Business of throwing away dead white carnations. It seemed vaguely indecent just to chuck them in the rubbish and ring the whistle for William and shoot them down the dumb waiter.

Pa and Ma Traphagen staying on to see a little something of the city. Fanny complacent in gray silk and Abram stooped with the weight of his heartache for "a noble man struck in his prime", for "Dide" and for the "fatherless babes". He was banal, but they were the only phrases he knew.

Ida emerging from her semi-paralysis to realize that Arthur's sisters were planning to send the children through college. They would take over the entire responsibility of their beloved brother's offspring. Little Marjorie was ready now. Wouldn't the University of Michigan be best, where they themselves had starved and studied? The educational atmosphere was so sound.

The immediate menace roused Ida as nothing else would have done. The earth had gaped beneath her. The support she had taken as much for granted as air and water had gone out from under her. She was left alone with a young boy and a young female egoist, to fight the fight. Here was assistance. But it was help from the enemy's camp. Her daughter would be in the hands of women dedicated to high doctrines of mind and soul—women unfashionable and unworldly. With a terrific effort of will she rallied her wits to refuse them. It was a fight, not only for life, but for her dreams. Whipped, frightened, solitary, she hoisted her flag above her tent and crept out bleeding, to stand them off.

Thank you, Wilmer. Thank you Madeline. Thank you, Grace. But she could manage very nicely. Arthur had insurance, you know. No mention of the fact that it would scarcely cover outstanding bills. They didn't need to fear that Arthur's children would be denied the higher education. And there was the farm, of course. Oh yes, the farm.

The Battle

If Arthur Kinnan, at his death, had left a non-paying railroad or unworked mines, his wife would have done as she did with his tragic two hundred and forty acres of old Maryland soil. She plunged into an analysis of the situation with a business acumen born seemingly full fledged from her courage and her need. She went over her husband's careful farm records. In the year just ended, he had come out exactly even. The income from cream, milk, hay, and sale of young stock had balanced almost to the dollar against farm expenditures. In another year, the place, now trim and neat with its red barns, its silo, its immaculate dairy and prosperous cows, would have made a return. Dimly, she could see the outlines of his dream. He was making it come true out of worn-out soil and the sacrifice of his body. Could she materialize her dream from a fresh life and the sacrifice of hers? Arthur's dream—Hers—. He may have come closer than she, when all was said and done. She was assailed with regrets for her obstructionism. She might have compromised a little more. She had been so harsh, fighting for her plans.

Her plans—. She sank into despair. Was anyone else, she wondered, full of such folly? Did everyone fight foolishly to build a dream? What was there to live for, otherwise? When she had done the best she could for the girl, yes, and for the boy, too, she prayed to the God she did not believe in that she might find a little corner in which to rest a while, and die.

Then she would be suffused with fresh hope. If her daughter made the success of life she was scheming for, surely she would find life sweet again.

She went on foot through the country around the farm, finding out property values. Arthur had placed a high valuation on his land, for future speculation—and because he did not really care to sell. There was no market for farm land *per se.* Armada Farm was surrounded by land for sale. True, adjoining it just across Rock Creek were the fine farms of Rear Admiral Selfridge and of Fond and Graham; rich men, all of them, who made hobbies of them. Rich men? Rich men seldom had hobbies without point, she had noticed. They had a way of turning over their playthings at a pretty profit. She engaged the superintendents of the hobbies in talk. She asked this question and that. She made shrewd deductions. Finally she reached the rumor, the merest breath, that a syndicate of Washington and Pittsburgh men planned some day, to build a highway between the two cities, following a line north up Rock Creek that would take in the Kinnan property.

For a rash moment she was tempted to go out to the farm and run it herself. In the shape it was now in, with her girlhood knowledge of farm ways, she could make a living on it for herself and her children. It would take care of them, and she could gamble against time for the sure growth of Washington, of innumerable highways, that would turn the ten-mile-distant acres into a suburban development. The richest push of the city was that way. Up the Rock Creek that made a picture park in the heart of the city. Up the Rockville Pike. Some day—and she had called her husband a fool!—those acres would make somebody wealthy. The highway might or might not go through. But money was there.

But it meant, for the girl, no college; or college under the influence of

the aunts. For the boy, the drudgery of a farm lad. For herself, the plod-
ding walk back an old road again; back to the making of butter and the
carrying of buttermilk to hogs. Better the other way, the way she had
first planned.

She had gleaned that the director of the Pan-American Union was
among those interested in the Pittsburgh-Washington project. She
pinned on her worn hat and brushed her best coat and walked like a
soldier across the marble floors and through the stately pillars of the
great Pan-American building. She sent in her calling card, relic of old
days. She scratched out the "Tuesday" which indicated her day "At
Home" and wrote "In reference to the Pittsburgh-Washington highway". In astonishment, the great man had her ushered in at once. This
thing was not known. Its development was so far distant that it was not
desirable that it be known. Who was this Mrs. Arthur Frank Kinnan
who was at home on Tuesdays? She came in and sat down calmly, a lean,
immaculate woman with shrewd eyes and shabby clothes. She stated her
case with the few words of an old financier.

Since her husband's death recently, she owned such and such a parcel
of land, lying so and so between Rock Creek, the railroad and Rockville
Pike. She wished to dispose of it, and had reason to believe that he, or
his friends, might be interested in it solely because of its location. Her
husband had held it at such and such a price. Her distinguished auditor
tapped his pencil on his massive desk. He was filled with respect for this
plain, bony widow. Jove, he had men working for him without half her
understanding. Where had she unearthed her information?

She had other properties? He knew too much about people to let her
appearance mislead him too far astray as to her circumstances. No, no
other property. She had a family? Yes, two children. A girl ready for
college. Indeed?

If she would excuse him he would telephone a friend. A friend in the real estate business. It was highly possible that a purchaser might be found for her land, at a reasonable figure. As she herself had pointed out, it was valueless except for its location. The value of that too was chimerical.

After another call, with the added presence of the friend in the real estate business, an offer was made her for her farm. The figure was well under her husband's but several times its cost to him and its actual agricultural worth.

She accepted it. At the close of the transaction, she disgraced herself and shocked the gentlemen by bursting into tears. Since her husband's death, her nerves had lain like antennae exposed to every touch. She had controlled herself to the last minute. The gentlemen bowed her out with a puzzled wonder.

Her six per cent income was just enough to carry her. Life would be lived in layers; cream for Marjorie, skimmed milk for the boy; for herself, she would have to add water to the bottom of the cup.

She finished out the months from January to June in the apartment. She managed new spring clothes for the girl, as usual. When they looked at hats for her, they both became enamored of a bright red one. They agreed that it was the most becoming hat she had ever tried on. Ida said, "But don't you think it's a little bright, under the circumstances?"

The girl laid it away, lingeringly, and chose another without enthusiasm. All spring, Ida regretted that she hadn't let her buy the red one. Arthur wouldn't have minded. She came within an ace of going back after it, but her cash was running low.

The girl's graduation went forward as though nothing had happened. The white dress was made of silk chiffon when cotton voile might have answered. Ida sent anonymous flowers, for fear there might not be others. The two of them came back to the apartment together and looked over the assortment of gifts and flowers. The girl turned away to hide her tears. Ida whispered, "Isn't it awful—" and they held each other close. Ida stroked her hair awkwardly.

"You do care a little about me, don't you? You aren't ashamed of me all the time? Your father used to say to you—you know you're even more mine—it's truer of the mother 'blood of my blood'—." Her voice broke. The girl drew away a little.

"Of course I care about you. But don't be sentimental."

In June, Ida held her auction of the stock and equipment of the farm. She went about it as efficiently as though she had been holding country sales all her life. She wrote her advertisements for the small newspapers of Rockville and Frederick. "All the registered stock of Armada Farm at your own price." She shopped Pennsylvania Avenue for the cheapest job printer to turn out a thousand sale announcements. She hired a horse and buggy at Rockville and drove around a twenty-mile radius tacking them to trees and telegraph poles and fences. She hired the best auction-eer in the country, and let it be known that refreshments would be pro-vided free for those spending the day.

She allowed the tears to flow for Redmon's benefit. He shifted his cud and pulled his red mustache and assured her that she could count on him. Yes'm, he knew what she meant about not going back on her. He curried every mule, every horse, every cow; polished the heifers until their spotted coats shone; at the risk of his life corraled the venerable bull, DeKol Second's Paul DeKol, No 2's Ormsby, and brushed his tail.

At dawn, Ida was up in the apartment, making ham sandwiches by the market basket. The girl could not endure to go to the auction. It seemed sacrilege to her. She had been in favor of keeping the farm and living on it. Ida and little Arthur carried the great baskets to the Rockville trolley. Redmon met them at the other end with the farm wagon, washed clean, with new red spokes to its wheels—his own idea.

The auction was the greatest success in the history of the county. The well-groomed stock brought fancy prices. Redmon's red spokes brought spirited bidding. Arthur's prize herd of cattle that he had gathered so slowly, at such cost, was dispersed. Twilight saw the new owners leading them away, lowing, with new Manila ropes. Little Arthur and Willy Redmon had done a land office business selling the free sandwiches at ten cents apiece.

Over five thousand dollars on Redmon's kitchen table, in cash and notes. The income-bearing farm notes safe in the bank. If she had had her way, these long eight years, it would all have been on Marjorie's back and in vague "advantages". They would have had nothing. Now, by playing safe, she was secure. She wouldn't spend a penny of her principal, and there would be a nice little nest egg for the children when she was through with the use of it. Perhaps by that time Marjorie would be a famous novelist or married to a young governor, and wouldn't even need it. Still, a few thousands would be nice for her in any case—.

Ida paid off Redmon. He gathered up his family and set out for Rockville, where the unknown waited for them and good hot liquor for him. The poplar leaves sifted across the porch of the farm house. The grass grew deep in the locust grove. The cardinals were thicker in the sycamores by the Creek. When Ida went back five years later, the long rows of stalls lay idle, the unpainted timbers of the barns were beginning to decay, and the wild dewberry vines and the Queen Anne's lace had taken over the fields of grain. Arthur's dream had taken form and had faded again into limbo.

In August 1914, Ida shipped off her furniture to Madison, Wisconsin, and followed with her children in time for Marjorie to enroll in the University. It was like going to the end of the world, after years of Washington, but she wished it were further. There was nothing here any more for any of them. The expensive women's colleges were out of the question. Of Marjorie's school mates, the boys were going on to Harvard and Princeton and Annapolis. The girls were preparing for Wellesley and Smith, for marriage, for their débuts. The Kinnan's might as well move on without the humiliation of being forgotten on the home grounds.

Wisconsin? Yes, the English department was said to be very fine. Marjorie would want that, in preparation for her career. The school stood higher than at any time until the Presidency of Glenn Frank, for the LaFollette prestige ran high and made it much talked of. A fresh start, that was the thing. They would get along better in a territory where class distinctions were not shaved wafer thin. Perhaps Marjorie could come back to Washington in time for her to see—rich and beautifully dressed and famous. When Marjorie did go back, it was only to pass through on her way to the south to take up farming with her husband, and Ida was not there to see or know.

The town of Madison was to Ida a little haven of delight. All the nice things of life were here in miniature; the capitol activity, the pretty homes, the well-to-do families. The swarms of students were lively and gay. They did not have the dignity of Washington young folk, but that too was just as well. On a sunny September day, with the whitecaps bobbing on Lake Mendota, she climbed the steep incline of "The Hill" to the group of old buildings, cream-weathered, ivy-dressed, that looked down on lake, on town, across to the Capital, that were to house her daughter and her hopes. She stepped across the threshold of Main Hall, staring about her with pleased interest. There was a half-snarl behind her. Her daughter was stamping her foot and pouting surlily. It seemed that as the one who, after all, was going to attend this institution, she should have gone first across the sacred portals.

"It's just a symbol," she said loftily.

To Ida, too, it had been a symbol. She dropped back, subdued her comments and her interest, and tagged the girl about over the campus grounds, wilted and dispirited.

It was a thankless task, this getting started. She didn't want to bother Marjorie with details, for she was rapt with her daily discoveries. She didn't want her to be conscious of any financial lack, either, but the line must be drawn when the girl unearthed the most expensive apartments in the town and begged for one. The choice of homes narrowed down to a small apartment in a poor side street that they could afford, and a large one on Lake Mendota in a good section, that they could not. Ida leased the expensive one, and rented two of the bedrooms to student girls. She could make a better showing, even with this social handicap, and she planned to say languidly, "With such an enormous apartment for the three of us, it seemed wrong not to let a couple of nice girls into the family, when space in Madison is at such a premium."

For eight years she went about saying, "It seemed wrong not to let two such nice girls into the family—"

Surreptitiously she cleaned the rooms of the two nice girls, keeping the pretense as long as possible that she had hired it done. The apartment being on the first floor, with a secluded rear giving on an enclosed yard, she found it possible to do her own washing without being observed by any of the students. All these corners must be turned that Marjorie might have fifteen dollar hats and a velvet suit, party dresses and slippers to match each one; money to spend. The books were so expensive. Marjorie didn't like to use second hand books, so they must all be new. Five dollars. Four. Three and a half. Well, Ida didn't want her to use old books, either. Heaven knew who might have had them last. She wore thick cotton stockings so that Marjorie might wear Italian silk.

Ida's day began early for Arthur's school was on the other side of town and he must get a good start. It was hard to get the girl up in time for her first classes and see that she was properly dressed. She was slovenly if not closely watched. She made a late dash for her class, and Ida had a cup of rich chocolate ready for her to drink in a hurry. Ida made it fresh when she was sure the girl was out of bed to stay and poured it back and forth from cup to cup until the temperature was agreeable for quick drinking. Sometimes the girl dashed out of the front door without coming out to the kitchen at all, and Ida poured the chocolate back and forth until it was cold, only to go in at the continued silence and find the girl had gone without a word.

She worked feverishly until mid-afternoon, so that when the girl came home from her last class, Ida would be free to sit down and listen to everything that had happened that day. It took all her morning to tidy up the place, to pick up and look over the girl's clothes, to wash or iron, to prepare lunch, for both children came home at noon. The boy had entered high school. They both ate hurriedly and dashed away again. Or Marjorie was all tired out and lay down after lunch with a book. Then when she had finished the lunch dishes, she changed her gingham work dress for street clothes and went down town to market. It was a daily outing she enjoyed to the full. The streets full of students calling to one another, running down the sidewalks with a pretense of haste, guffawing on the corners, the girls in arm-linked groups of twos and threes and sometimes a whole sorority at times, laughing and rolling their eyes sideways for glimpses of boys they knew; it was tremendously exhilarating. The whole atmosphere was vibrant with youth and hope. Anything might happen to these vivid young creatures with the air of conquerors. She came home with her cheeks pink and tingling from the crisp Wisconsin air. When she had too many bundles, she slipped in the back way, through Mrs. Frawley's back yard.

She waited anxiously for news from the battle front. The classes were going nicely. Marjorie was placed after the first week of trial in the advanced composition class of William Ellery Leonard, an honor that was only to be expected. She reported that Leonard called her to him and trailed his long finger across her first essay.

"You have a most impressive vocabulary for a girl of your age," he said in his nasal intonation. "I presume you're young," casting a half contemptuous eye up and down her. "I can't always tell."

The girl neglected to add that he had further trailed his pencil across her paper, flicking down adjectives and destroying adverbs by the dozen.

"Too damn impressive," he had snorted.

The girl brought home delighted tales of his genius and his insults that filled Ida with dismay. His careful reading aloud of a callow composition was interrupted one day by the sudden guffaw of a male student at its patent absurdity. Leonard threw down the paper and stormed up and down in front of his rostrum like DeKol Second Paul DeKol pawing and bellowing to break loose from his pen. His black eyes flashed, his classical nose was white with rage, he shook his luxuriant mane in a frenzy.

"We were getting along very nicely until some braying jackass entered the room!" he roared.

No other professor in the University would have dared—or cared—to call a student a braying jackass. Marjorie said she thought it was delicious, but to Ida it was most unseemly. If the girl were not working under him with so evident a stimulation, she would have been even more distressed. She was afraid he had wild, free ideas.

He ordered Marjorie to write a short story without an adjective or adverb in its pages. She had protested. Her stock in trade was her adjectives and adverbs. That was just the point. They were running away with her and would soon break her neck for her.

"But Mr. Leonard," she wailed, "it just can't be done."

"And I say it can!" he bellowed. "I guess I ought to know more about adjectives and adverbs than a chit of a schoolgirl!"

Ida mourned with her over the impossible harshness of the order, but Marjorie reported that it was indeed possible. She had been forced to concoct a stark plot, about stark people, and call it "The Brute". But by the use of heavy nouns and verbs, the impression could be conveyed, the story told. It had no value except as an exercise, but it was far above her customary precocious babbling. Ida considered it execrable.

"I like your other things so much better. You always have such beautiful descriptions."

Leonard said of it, "That's better. Your things are usually crawling with words."

Ida said, "But Marjorie, he's insulting. I don't call that encouragement."

Marjorie insisted, "It's encouraging for him to give me that much attention. He wouldn't bother with me at all if he thought I was hopeless." She was sulky that day and added "Sometimes I think that what I need is not encouragement, but killing; I can't write—"

These moods put Ida on pins and needles. Such talk was treason. Except that she saw the girl going at her writing with renewed vigor, she would have blamed Leonard bitterly for discouraging her. Pity that she could not see that a succession of Leonard's would have been the only thing to save the girl. The later professors were "darlings"—but they were too lenient.

Ida feared all radical influences. All unconventionality was anathema. That was the way of the Kinnan's, wild of talk and wilder of dress. She heard with misgiving the tales of scandal with which Leonard was persecuted. The old wives waggled their heads and spun their yarns. He had driven his poor wife crazy with his cruelty. He had thrown all the teacups at her head one morning. He might better have murdered her out-right. He was bad. He was crazy. He was this, that, and the other. After his wife's suicide he had begun "going after" Helen K——, a mere child. Her family, where he had long been a friend, had been forced to forbid him the house. It was necessary to threaten him, if he should ever come near her again. Ida agreed that it was quite right to drive him out. She shuddered at the thought of "such a man" pursuing her own daughter. She supposed that in a professorial capacity, he was comparatively harm-less, except for his ideas. When Helen became Marjorie's friend, a differ-ent story was told. A story of a genius, half mad with despair, seeking out for his mental comfort the mature ease of her beautiful mind. She was young enough to listen to him. They rambled around the lovely lakes while he relieved himself of his pain and his poetry. The experi-ence was a spiritual soaring for the girl. When her family brutalized the affair, she had been permanently hurt and shocked. It reminded Mar-jorie of Rafe Redmon and her mother's pointed finger.

Marjorie seized on Leonard's exquisite dedication to his dead wife of one of his volumes, closing

"My poems, all my sacred best of life,

Be yours, forever—oh, my wife, my wife!"

She read it to Ida with tears in her eyes. Ida shook her head. "It's all very well to write poems." When two tales are told—believe the bad.

Ida could never pass the man on the street without seeing him throw-ing imaginary teacups at his wife. He was married again, to a blue-eyed philosopher—"God pity her" said the old wives—and Ida often saw him stalking homeward with a little bag of candy in his hand. Half of his mind was in the clouds with his thundering gods, the other half glared defiantly at his persecuting world. He strode along with a thick coonskin cap ludicrous above his handsome face—a hounded Byron taking home a bag of peppermints.

Socially, the girl was not making progress. It was not to be wondered at, for they knew no one, had no letters, nothing. Ida felt that she was putting too much of the burden on the girl. She would have to make her own place. There was no other way. There were several Washington acquaintances of the girl at the University, who called dutifully, but here with their new friends and interests there was no reason for giving her an attention they had never given her before. Ida felt maddeningly helpless. If it would have done the least good, she would have walked up and down "The Hill" with placards like a sandwich man, advertising her daughter. She waited nervously for Marjorie to begin to "make friends".

Every well-dressed girl was given sorority attention, and she received rushing invitations from four groups. The two inferior ones "bid" her at once. She sensed their rating and refused. Of the two highly desirable groups, one rejected her cursorily. She had overplayed her hand.

"Let them think you were somebody in Washington" Ida admonished the girl as she left for the rushing dinner.

The girl laid it on thick. Her table companion at her left admitted she knew something of Washington and asked innocent questions. Marjorie threw famous names about recklessly. She was not asked to this house again, and long afterward discovered that her questioner had been the daughter of a most distinguished congressman, wealthy, of high social prestige, who had trapped her in her cheap pretense at every turn.

Marjorie cried bitterly over this. She had had a trick for some years, under Ida's tutelage, of "giving a good impression". It had been her undoing. She learned a bitter lesson, not quite soon enough.

The remaining sorority, to which she was greatly drawn, was more patient. They too felt constrained at last to refuse her. Their reasons were two: a quite insufferable cockiness in the girl; and the jejune assort-ment of high school pins which she wore plastered on her breast. There were eight or nine of them, gold, and silver and enamel, stars and Maltese crosses and bars and squares. The two girls who had sponsored her invitations worked slyly to have her remove them. But she refused proudly. They were her badges of honor.

The withheld bids were good for her, as Leonard's insults were good. But Ida suffered acutely. When the girl began to realize that the climb was long and uncertain to any sort of recognition in this great University; when decent doubts as to what life owed her overcame her; the improvement in her was apparent to anyone.

The girl said, "I don't need a sorority. I don't need anything. I can make my way on my own feet."

"That's very brave—" Ida replied. But in her heart she thought, "You don't know. The things I want for you are based on sororities and parties and men—you just don't know."

Later when the high school pins and some of the cockiness dropped from sight, and the girl received the bid she had wanted so desperately a few months before, she was able to put the honor in its proper place. Membership in a sorority was pleasant and made life at school simpler and more gracious. But in her suffering at the slight, she had been able to pass beyond the need of things like this. The bid and its acceptance picked Ida up from the abyss over which she had been hovering and put her on firm ground. Now she could fight with renewed spirit. It would have been more than she could endure, to have the girl living here, as she had, in Washington, on the fringes of life. Not quite accepted. Not quite good enough. If she trusted her daughter's ability at all, she need not have been disturbed. There was room in the generosity of this place for anyone with the smallest talent. There was prestige for anyone who worked, and there were enough young men and enough parties, almost, for everybody.

It was the matter of selection among the young men that brought to light Ida's willingness to compromise with truth. It was "for her daughter's sake", but the girl was shocked. Then she too accepted the new standard and lied quite calmly for the rest of her University life.

Ida had started her out with the respectable Michigan notion that a girl told the truth about her engagements with men to other men. The first young man who invited her out for a certain evening was necessarily accepted, be he lame, halt or blind. The telephone would ring. Ida enjoyed answering it and seeing if she could recognize the voice—she could temper the disappointment for Marjorie too if it was only a girl. Then as she overheard the girl's conversation she could share it in thought.

"Why no, Mr. Woodward, I'm not busy then. Yes, indeed, I'd just love to go."

The phraseology was standard.

Most of her week-end dates were absorbed at the start by the activities of the Dixie Club, a shoddy little affair of queer Southerners, for the most part. It was not until later that she realized that students only bothered with these odd little organizations when none other was offered them. They were not "big time".

A certain Friday had been dated up weeks ahead for a Dixie Club dance at a cheap hall. A week in advance, a new voice on the telephone asked for Miss Kinnan. Ida heard her daughter say:

"Oh yes, Mr. Williams, I remember meeting you at the house reception. Yes indeedy. The fourteenth? Oh, I'm so sorry. I'm going to the Dixie Club dance with Murray L—."

Mr. Williams evidently closed the conversation hastily. Marjorie turned from the phone, puzzled, to report to headquarters that he had said "Oh, My God! Thank you, Miss Kinnan," and had hung up.

Ida would have liked to hold the theory that his great disappointment accounted for the phrase. But as the days went on and he did not call again, she engaged in confidences with one of Marjorie's most popular sorority sisters.

The sister was overcome at Mrs. Kinnan's revelations.

"Oh, Mrs. Kinnan, I'm so glad you told me these things. Why, it might have *ruined* Marge! She just doesn't understand."

It seemed that Mr. Williams was the biggest, best-looking member of the most desirable, pretentious fraternity on the campus. On the fourteenth, as anyone who kept their ears open should have known, his fraternity was giving its fall formal, a dinner and dance. Why, any girl in school, let alone a freshman, would give her ears to go. Murray L— was an undersized little fellow of total insignificance and a member of one of the rottenest fraternities in school. This was awful!

Mr. Williams had said "Oh, My God!" to think that he, himself, was engaged in competition with the Dixie Club and Murray L—. He was terribly fussy about the girls he took out. It was a shame, but he'd never ask Marge again.

It seemed that the "boobs" always asked for dates weeks and months ahead. They had to. The eligibles called on shorter notice. They could do it. It appeared that when a boob telephoned, he was told regularly, "I'm so sorry, but I'm all dated up for weeks and weeks. Call me again." It was all right to have them telephone because it added to the general air of popularity. When just an average fellow called, it was well to stall for time until you found out whether he wanted you just to drop into a Candy Shop dance or whether his fraternity had something on worthwhile. When he asked if you were busy on the ninth, you said, teasingly:

"Oh now, don't you wish you knew? Why, what's on, Bill?"

If it was "Oh, nothing much", it was wiser, if it was far enough ahead of time, to be "awfully sorry, but I do have a date that night, Bill, but don't you forget me, will you?"

If any of the real men, the "W" men, the big men, the Adonises and the Apollos, any of the leaders, wanted a date, even at the last minute, break your old date as if it didn't exist. Unless you were dated up with a pretty regular fellow who thought a lot of you. Then it didn't pay to get all balled up with him. The date-breaking story was:

"Bill, I got so mixed up on this week's dates that I don't know where I'm going. What time was that date I had with you? The tenth, wasn't it? What, the ninth? Oh, Bill, you must be mistaken. I've got you down for the tenth. I promised what's-his-name, Jimmy Atkins, the ninth, just ages and ages ago——"

But you had to know what was on at all the houses for certain nights and try to keep clear ahead of time for anything good you might be asked to. Then as the week went on, you dated up with almost anybody for the nights you didn't have filled. You must dance somewhere every Friday and Saturday.

And never, never, did you tell another man with whom else you were going out on a set date, unless it was someone perfectly marvelous and you wanted it told and didn't intend to break the engagement. Of course, sometimes you got into awfully hot water and had to lie like everything to fix it up. Sometimes you lost a man altogether if he found you out. But you just had to be clever about it——.

After long thought Ida saw the wisdom of this course. A girl had to protect herself against the poor devils looking for girls to go out with. No reason why Marjorie should be the victim. Her first months had been a succession of male atrocities who dated early. In due time, she encouraged her daughter "just to be clever about it" and complacently heard her inquire:

"Oh Slim, I just called up to see if I have a date with you this week. I'm all mixed up—"

As the college years slipped on, and the girl made herself more and more a part of the social life, achieved her little literary and dramatic honors, leads in plays, the writing of school plays, editorships on class publications and the intellectual "Lit", Ida felt that her life's work would surely reach justification. She was in her glory, planning stage and party costumes. She engaged a good dressmaker for six weeks in autumn and three in spring. She paid any price for a hat or suit or for materials. She wore her own cheap tailored suit for three years, and an unbecoming black velvet hat with a green bird became almost a fixture on her. She was recognized at far distances by the green bird.

Marjorie fell in love with a pair of gray kid shoes in a shop window. Marjorie said "Why, we can't pay a price like that for shoes, can we?" Ida said defiantly "I don't know why not. I can't dress you very much longer and I want the pleasure of doing it right. These will be darling with your new blue crepe."

As the girl followed her mother out of the shop, tripping ecstatically in the new shoes, her eye dropped to the bottom of her mother's right foot as it turned its sole up in her stride. There was a hole worn through shoe and stocking to the bare, callused foot.

The girl had her moments of balance. Rare as they were, they reassured Ida that her daughter did appreciate all she was doing for her. She said angrily now, "Mother you bought me these extravagant shoes and you're showing the skin through yours."

Ida said calmly, "I know it. I've put off getting new ones because my feet are so sore and I can't bear the thought of stiff new shoes."

But for the most part the girl took in greedily everything her mother tendered; dropped her nightgown and soiled underwear on the floor of her room for her mother to bend her back over. Ida tried to have her wash her own silk stockings, but gave it up. She asked nothing more of her, except a little dusting on Saturday morning. That was, naturally, if the girl was not asleep after a dance the night before or deep in the throes of a literary "inspiration". Then Ida tiptoed around and did her work quietly, oiling the carpet sweeper so that it wouldn't squeak, sweeping softly against the door sill like a nibbling mouse. Nine times out of ten, she sometimes suspected, the girl lay there wide awake.

But she didn't mind. A girl was only young once and she wanted a free, happy girlhood to be her daughter's preparation for her later life of ease. She didn't intend to teach her to cook or keep house.

"If you don't know how," she reasoned, "you're much less apt to have to do it. It would simply kill me if I thought you were ever going to have to slave the way I've done."

The girl poo-poohed: "You don't have to slave. You're too particular. Who cares whether this apartment is spotless."

But one evening, after Ida had had one of her headaches, the girl made quite a stew when she found the living room thick with dust.

Now and then Ida had opportunities to make friendships of her own. Here and there a woman of intellect found a challenge in the starkness of this woman, who fought life so courageously and allowed her daughter to be rude to her in public. There was a good mind buried there, they thought. A summer student, a teacher from Smith, who was one of the two nice girls during the summer session, dug at her vigorously during her sojourn.

"Why haven't you encouraged your mother to take some classes at the University?" she raged at the daughter. "She has a splendid mind. She only needs to study and to know."

The idea of her mother in the quest of knowledge seemed absurd. It was too late in life for her to begin. Ida didn't want anything like that for herself. She was too busy, anyway. She only had a little time in the evening, and then she was too tired.

The wife of a member of the Philosophy Department who lived on the Court, groped for her. She felt that a fine woman was here, a profound woman, strangely polluted by inferior standards of life. Why did she dress the snip of a daughter so beautifully and go shabby herself? Why didn't she pay more attention to herself? She wasn't an individual, but a slave, but something was there—some hidden force, some burning power. Men and women of perception were conscious of it. She had indeed a gift for battle. She had only dedicated it to unworthy ends. As an egotist, for such indeed she was, she would have fared better to have fought for herself. There would not have been the torment in living her own life, that she experienced in trying to live her daughter's.

For her daughter was getting away from her. She accepted slight after slight from her, in order not to press the issue. She was only the background in the tapestry of this girl's life. But never mind, she herself had woven the design. She was content, until the battle was won and the girl on the road to glory, to fall asleep by the lamp in the evening, and wake up at midnight in time to unlock the door for the incoming dancer and take the confidences, the relaying of compliments and conquests that were the crumbs on which she fed. There would be later years, when she had done her work, and the boy's and girl's diplomas hung on the wall, when she could rest and rest; and have her nails done, and her hair; have a silk nightgown, if she wanted it, and sleep until noon; live quietly on her income, perhaps in Fenton, where she could be quite the lady; save a little and travel a little; spend part of the year with her rich and famous daughter, dressed elegantly to meet her daughter's friends. She would spend some time with the boy, too, wherever he might be, whatever he might be doing, if he were not married; and in the months when she was comfortably alone, she would have those good fat letters from her daughter, fat with success, to start off her day of ease. When her work was done—

But it was not yet done. And the girl was talking crazy philosophical talk and trampling over her mother, body and soul, and beginning to run with a queer, intellectual bunch. There had come the time, in her life, when she was filled with the usual juvenile despair at life's futility. Ida did not know that at this time youth chooses its subsequent philosophy; permanent despair, courage; retreat into the herd, into the utmost possible mediocrity; or finds a renewed appetite for the adventure of living.

The girl said gloomily, "I have been considering suicide—"

She wanted, naturally, to be told how valuable her life was—But Ida instead, in a wave of self pity, reproached her with her ingratitude.

"After all I've done for you—"

The girl turned on her venomously.

"I owe you nothing. I haven't the slightest respect for your sacrifices. You forced life on me and I'm not sure whether it's a gift worth having. I don't respect you, because you don't have any self-respect. You've given me all these fine clothes you're throwing up to me now. I'd like you better if you'd put some of them on your own back and not keep me ashamed of you, sneaking in the back way, in your dingy old duds.

"You think you've been unselfish. You haven't. You've been one of the most selfish mothers I know anything about, because you've made me try to live the way you want me to instead of the way that appeals to me. Your own life was a failure and when you're egging me on to do things and be somebody and keep a lot of silly boys running after me, you're trying to have me make up for the things you couldn't do. You say you've stood everything from me—abuse. Why shouldn't you stand it? I'm your last chance at life.

"You fuss at me to write, to write. Then when I do, you criticize it if it isn't sweet and pretty. You're wrapped up in what people think and I despise—it."

There were times, such as this, when Ida hated her child. She was so alien. She hated herself for having lived in her. She sobbed,

"If I'd only known what I know now, I'd never have had you, I'd never have had you. It hasn't been worth the effort—"

"It's a little bit late to make up your mind," the girl sneered. "Bah!"

Ida dissolved into tears. She wouldn't stand it. She couldn't stand it.

"I'm going away," she sniffled. "You can just get along the best you can without me."

"What are you going to do?" inquired the girl coldly. "Kill yourself?"

"Just go away—"

She groped for the hat with the green bird, picked up her shabby purse mechanically and drew on her jacket as she went blindly out of the door.

The thoughts of youth are long, long thoughts, but youth's tempests are brief. The raw mind, irritated by life, frets itself into an outburst of mad ideas of madder words. The adolescent storm beats in—and then is gone. Life is good again. There is courage and to spare. The girl calmed down. Of course life was worth living. Of course she would make a success of it. No one could feel such strength and exuberance as hers and fail to make a success. She was not afraid of anything.

Poor, homely mother. She did despise her but she shouldn't be so mean to her. She shouldn't be so mean to Arthur. How mad he had been the night he had asked her, with his most gentlemanly air, to go to the movies; and when he was all ready, with money in his pockets from the newspapers he got up at four in the morning to peddle, the telephone had rung and she had gone off with a college fellow. She really wouldn't have gone if she'd known the kid's feelings would be so hurt. He'd lost all confidence in her. And just as she was beginning to be a little fond of him. She must be more careful. She took great satisfaction in treading on the family toes. She'd be a good girl and make everybody love her. Her mood grew quite angelic.

She regretted having been so blunt with Mother. Could she possibly have meant it about running away? And where would she go and what would she do? She opened the door and peered out. A fine rain was falling through the darkness. The tinny piano in the Beta house across the way was muted by its soft rustle. The telephone rang. When she went to the back of the house again, Ida sat in a chair in the far corner of the kitchen, spent and haggish, wet to the skin. Her hair straggled under the wing of the green bird, her nose was red from weeping, her eyes and lips were swollen out of shape. She looked appealingly at her daughter—defeated. She had been too lonely. She could not endure the isolation. She had returned like a dog to the insults, to further sacrifices, in order to have another chance at living that young life.

In her hand was a wet bag of a quarter's worth of chocolates. She had made this pitiful gesture of independence. She held up the bag. "I meant to eat them all alone, eat them all up" she said.

The girl kissed her out of pure pity. She felt young and strong and superior.

"Now Mother, don't act silly about the things I say. I have to talk and rave once in a while. That's where you're so foolish. You shouldn't take me so seriously—"

Ida shook her head dumbly, as if to say, "Never mind. Don't let's argue again. Just never mind—"

She held out the wet bag.

"Here—they're pretty good."

The girl carried them away with her to her studies.

It was easy to fall back into picking up the nightgown and the underwear and pouring the hot chocolate from one cup to another. Pleasanter to forget than to remember. Easy to fall back into the Lethe of the old dreams. After her ugly outbursts, the girl would have spells of sweetness, or bring home trophies that could not but appease her mother. Phi Beta Kappa, a prize in Union Vodvil. The thrill of seeing her child—hers, moving behind the footlights, her name on programs. The invitation by both parties to run for vice president on their tickets—the "trick" poem that was "almost" accepted by *Century*. The note from William Rose Benét. The note from the *Atlantic Monthly*. "These verses have an arresting rhythm. We return them with especial thanks." All, all of it, sops to hope. A dozen others were taking off the same honors and doing sounder work. Esther Forbes, Mildred Evans, Carol McMillan. They made no pretenses and thought of other things.

The encouragement of Thomas H. Dickinson, with his faun's ears.

"I'm not commercially minded, but it seems to me this story would sell."

Words Ida had awaited feverishly—

But harassed college professors judge the little essays and the little stories by college standards. What else is there to do? One cannot hold up adolescent gropings against the white curtain of the masters. A separate standard is held up, and in the welter of young awkwardness the glib composition is praised.

It was Dickinson again, whose remark to her daughter delighted the mother. He was dancing with her at a function of the dramatic society.

"What are you, anyway?" he asked with his Pan-like quirk of the head. "An uncharted meteor?"

To Ida, it was the sort of "bouquet" she adored to have her daughter receive. But the girl frowned.

"I don't like it," she said slowly. "There's a sort of prophecy in it. A prophecy that I won't get anywhere."

"Mother," desperately, "You'll have to begin to stop thinking that I'm unique. There are so many of us with our dabby ability. Right in this school, so many of us—"

The Battle: Men

The greatest encouragement to Ida in her schemes was her daughter's attitude to men. They came by the law of averages in sufficient numbers to surround her with the aura of popularity, but Ida could see that their comings and goings were otherwise meaningless to the girl. She didn't want her to carry her indifference too far, but it was a great safety measure not to have her falling in and out of love, and perhaps engaging herself too young. Ida had a secret horror that the girl would marry as young as she had done, and "spoil her life".

There was a charming young instructor with whom the girl made an engagement for a Sunday morning walk. Ida fretted and fumed. A few hours before he was to come, she asked, "Marjorie, just how old is this teacher?"

The girl happened to know that he was twenty-eight.

Ida took it as an omen.

"Marjorie!" she cried. "That's just the age your father was when I married him! And a teacher too!"

It was not a coincidence. It was a menace. The man was probably just at the "marrying age". What would Marjorie do if he proposed to her?

"Lord, Mother, the man won't fall on my neck the first time I'm out with him."

"But your father practically proposed to me the first time he even asked to call."

"Well, what of it? You married him and lived happily ever after, didn't you? You loved him and wanted to marry him, didn't you?"

"Oh yes, certainly. But—"

"But what?"

"But you have a career to spoil. I want you to get started, make a name for yourself—you have it to do alone, you know—and then when you're in your late twenties, marry a governor!" She said it with whimsy, but in her heart it was really what she meant.

"Would you want to marry this poor teacher? Even engage yourself to him?"

She tormented the girl until she went to the telephone and broke the date with him. The man meant nothing to her, or she to him, and if she went out with him now, she would be fearfully self-conscious. Young instructors were more respectable than Rafe Redmon's, but they were just as great a danger, it seemed. For the rest of the year, a pained and puzzled young man heard her German quizzes.

The rest of them were safe; part of the brightness, the dance music, the canoe rides on the lake in the moonlight, the picnics, the dinners, the Proms and the house parties. Little Southern Woody, the most delightful of gentlemen, but so poor, so homely. He went in for American Beauties that he could not afford. Good old Dick, the best of friends. Marty and Fred, Fritz, the Milwaukee aristocrat, "Speed" the track man, Alvin and Hod and Gil and Kim. Nice safe boys who had to have some girl to take to dances. Now and then exotics showed up in the social flower garden like rank weeds.

There was "Gyp", tough and not very clean, son of a wealthy mayor of a small Wisconsin town. He had been in jail in towns other than his own and told of it. He laid siege to the girl violently. He said to Ida, who protested his taking Marjorie to dinner at the Park Hotel on a week night, "I know neither of you likes me but I don't care. I'm going to stick at it until you throw me out. I don't get to first base with her, but what of it? She may change her mind."

He brought the girl presents she could not accept, took her about in an expensive hired car. It seemed to Ida that at any moment he was likely to abduct the girl. Her mind was much relieved in 1917, when he went off to the war without so much as a farewell.

But from most of them there was nothing to fear, neither love nor marriage. She was only afraid that her daughter might be unduly harsh with any of them who became attached to her. The case of Ted reassured her. She sat drowsing in her daughter's room, waiting for her to come in from the pre-Prom dinner dance. There were voices at the door, the briefest "good night". The girl came in and dropped down on her bed, kicking off her high-heeled slippers.

"Well, Ted had to go and spoil the Prom," she said.

Ida's heart jumped. Had he "fallen" for some other girl, a not uncommon procedure?

"He proposed tonight, on the stairs, with people climbing up and down over us all the time. Lord!"

Another heart leap to a different rhythm.

"What did you do?"

"Oh, I was nice about it. Told him I didn't feel that way and when the excitement of Prom was over he probably wouldn't either. He said that with my literary ability and his undoubted medical genius, we should have marvelous children. Conceit! I wanted to scream, but he was so darned serious. You can't laugh in a man's face about his future children. I patted his hand and told him he deserved a fine wife, but one that would stay home and bring up his children. Now the rest of Prom will be a mess."

Ida was bursting with pride. It fitted so nicely into a long-cherished picture.

"I'm glad you were so gracious about it. I've been afraid you would be horrid to men who care for you, the way you were to Woody."

"Oh no. They're paying you a compliment of sorts."

Ida saw her off to Prom the next night with a full heart. Her daughter—in white pussywillow taffeta embroidered with gold, with her gold lace underskirt and gold slippers; violets at her waist; swishing off in a carriage with a fine young man she had graciously refused.

Mrs. Frawley, who kept the boarding house in the rear, phrased it differently to Mrs. Tompson, who kept the rooming house on the right: "Yes, I saw that Marjorie stepping off to the Prom in clothes that come right out of her mother's hide. Yes, with a young medical student, and much good it will do her."

Ida sat all night with a faint smile on her face, picturing every turn of the dance in the swish of the gold lace underskirt. By straining her ears, she fancied she could hear the music, down in the marble halls of the Capital. I dreamt I dwelled in marble halls. It was a thick, silent, snowy Wisconsin night. The fraternity houses about were still and dark, save where a student light here and there on a third floor shone on some youth too poor or too indifferent to attend the Prom.

Then in the early spring of 1918, the senior year, the catastrophe occurred. Out of the safe void, appeared a young man on crutches, to whom the girl addressed herself with the matter-of-fact tone she used around the house. None of the sprightliness, the gay affectations, the coyness, of her past relations with her beaus. Mildred, one of the two nice young girls of the season, who had indeed been taken into the family, smelled a rat in this tone of voice. The girl spoke to the young man with the broken leg as though she had known him all her life. As Ida soon understood, there was indeed the fatal recognition.

She was crushed. Her plans were little scraps of paper in a basket, and the March wind had upset it and scattered them to the end of the earth.

She wailed her objections. They were many. He didn't have a thing, did he? His people were just everyday people, weren't they?

He was on crutches this minute—he might be a cripple for life, and here she was planning to tie her life to his. It was insanity. Then she flung her final insult.

"I tell you Marjorie, he's mediocre."

The girl, poised for a moment on the fence, dropped at once to the other side and there was no further point in talk. If Ida couldn't see him as she did, let her look at both their backs. He summed up for her all she asked of life. He was the core of her puzzle, and the other jagged pieces would have to fit in around him. A thin steel wall dropped down between mother and daughter. The girl announced her engagement at dinner at his fraternity house without even informing her mother of her decision to do so.

Mildred, sick at heart for the lonely woman, hurried to Ida and lied. Chuck had urged Marjorie to make the announcement that day. Marjorie hadn't had time to see her mother, and had sent Mildred to tell her. She knew it was a lie, but it was easier to accept than to deny.

She sat by the living room window in the old reed chair, her hands folded in her lap. Banjos were plunking in the Beta house, the Delts were roaring with laughter, there was the clatter of silver and china. A belated Freshman ran madly by, late to dinner somewhere.

What was life doing to her anyway? Why was it turning on her so viciously at this stage of the game? She had heard others ask why life should abuse them, but they were souls who had asked nothing of life but to be let alone. Her case was different, she could see that. She had dared life, had fought it with her bare hands, to get the things she wanted. She had asked the things life is most perverse to withhold and most perverse to give.

There were other things—things that were only names to her. Things the Kinnan's, the queer Kinnan's, asked of life. Beauty—did they even know what they meant? Peace of soul—how could there be peace of soul with such a hunger and thirst as hers tormenting her? Love—God, love! The thing they called love was doing this to her daughter, doing this to her—taking her dreams from her, the excuse for existence from her. Beauty and peace and love—not worth the having! A hideous doubt assailed her. How could she be sure, when she had never known them?

When the girl came in, they stared at each other coldly. She rose and faced her.

"I began a fight for you," she said quietly, "more than twenty years ago. I've given my life to it and I don't intend to give in until the last hope is done. You're ashamed of me. You despise my mind. But you don't know what strength is. I'm not licked yet."

The next day she sent for "that young man". There was a session behind the closed doors of the living room. She seated him on the shabby old green davenport with the light in his face. "So that I can watch your eyes."

She told him what she asked of life for her daughter. If he would help her get them, or get them for her, well and good. But she wished to tell him frankly that she had no faith in him. He had waited to make sure his leg would heal, before he had spoken of his feeling to her daughter.

"That was very noble of you," she assured him cynically. "A man with one leg would have found it difficult to support a wife."

She flailed him unmercifully. If she could drive him off now, she would do it without compunction. Her daughter did not know what she was doing. It was her sacred duty to protect her.

"To protect her from what?" he queried grimly.

"From poverty. From mediocrity. From children wailing at her skirts. From sinking into the middle-class abyss—"

"Into which you brought her," he finished.

"I believe there are worse things than poverty and mediocrity," he went on, "and you exemplify them."

She had underestimated her adversary. He attacked her as cruelly as she had him.

"You are an evil, ambitious woman," he said. "You're greedy for the ugliest things in life. You've got a greedy, affected daughter, as selfish as Hell, and now I've got to undo some of your work to make her fit to live with. You've got her wanting the things you want. Money and clothes and society columns."

He shook his cane at her.

"You've tried to tell me how high a valuation you put on your daughter. And I tell you you hold her cheap. You'd sell her to the first dog with a million dollars."

It was now war to the finish, until one of them should admit defeat. Hate flamed like fire between them. It was worse than she had thought. He wanted the things the Kinnan's wanted—the beauty, the peace of soul, the love. The meaningless names.

She had an astonishing respect for him. No one, not even her daughter, had fought her like this. But he was more dangerous than in her deepest despair she had imagined. A thousand times more dangerous.

At Marjorie's graduation they sat side by side in a voluntary armistice. Side by side they sat on Ivy Day in the lovely outdoor theatre with the tall pines rustling and the sweet Wisconsin winds stirring across

Mendota below them. They listened, both stirred as always by the unexpected sound of the girl's voice, as she recited the class poem with an air of dedication. Ida's eyes filled with tears. She turned to the frowning young Viking beside her.

"I suppose," she whispered, "that even you will admit her talent. You can't deny the poem was beautiful."

He scowled and stamped his toe with his cane.

"I do deny it." He spoke aloud and the mother of the valedictorian, now speaking, turned around in horror from three rows away. "Terrible rot. Sentimental and cheap. She tossed it off yesterday afternoon. She's too damn sure of herself. Why, I'd rather write a poem that wouldn't even be read until after I was dead, and have it good, than a lifetime of trash that nit-wits would applaud."

She compressed her lips. She felt that only the hundreds of respectable mothers and fathers about her kept her from striking him.

Overture. Lights!

This then was the beginning of life. Here was the audience. The programs were rustling. The curtain quivered on the stage. There was a flutter in the proscenium. The orchestra struck up the overture. Lights!

Ida was in New York City with her daughter. Marjorie had come to knock on the portals of the great city. It was the fall of 1918, and the overgrown village was vital with the thrill of war. The girl was tip-toe with ecstasy. She longed to try her strength against these massive doors, to carve her initials on the substantiality of their insolent oak. Ida trailed her like a moth, trembling before the careless young flame of her. The flame that was to be removed from her sight; from her influence; from her will to fan or to blow out. The girl was armed with letters to Philip Littell of the *New Republic* and to Honore Willsie Morrow, from good Professor Dodge. The professor had seen too many of them come and go, the poets, the authors, the journalists, to offer her undue encouragement. Here were a couple of side doors to knock on. Only time and what was in her heart could tell. O. J. Campbell had only his blessing to give her. He grinned his pagan grin and said, oh, she'd get along alright. He was far more interested in her romance than in her verse. There was lots more meat in it.

The girl also had sufficient money for two or three months of unemployment. She had saved her odds and ends of literary prize money, and

Ida had capped the total with a like amount. It made a definite gamble, a poker player's challenge. Ida had called her daughter's hand.

"I'm seeing you. What have you got?"

She took the train back to Madison, where Arthur must be taken through four years more, sick at heart. She felt a tenderness for the girl herself, greater almost than ever before, now that she was seeing her leave the nest. If she could only fight the rest of the fight for her! Make that fatal appearance before the footlights! But at that, she didn't know where the strength would come from. She had just enough left to see the boy through and "encourage" the girl from the side lines. The girl was ready to take the battle up where she had left it. Perhaps the girl would prove strong enough even to overcome the handicap of marriage. Perhaps this threatened one wouldn't even go through. The young Viking was safely if temporarily at Camp Upton. He might go overseas, he might forget her, he might be killed. Just about so many young men had to be killed. He might die of the Spanish influenza. Just about so many soldiers had to die of it.

As the Twentieth Century ground and roared toward Chicago, she felt as though her body had been tied to a pillar in the New York station, and this irresistible mechanism was tearing it loose again. She was being divided self from self. Like a central knife edge in her pain, was the knowledge that to the girl the separation was only a relief.

She began the four years of Arthur's university life half-heartedly. All her mind was in New York following the girl from magazine office to office. It was only as her daughter drew further and further from her, that she turned to find the boy touching her humbly on the arm, ripe with a sweetness and a manliness she had never suspected, offering her his care and his affection. What then was this? She had made of her body, like Fabre's caterpillar, food for her young—but for her female young. The girl had battened on her and gone away, despising her. She had neglected the boy, ignored him. Here he was, a man, tendering her his love. What lesson was this? What was the caprice of life trying to teach her now? She turned to him for comfort, but it was with a widowed heart.

She "encouraged" the girl thus, in an early letter:

"Do you know, my dear, that it takes *conceit*, lots of it, gall, nerve, self-esteem, self-satisfaction, aggressiveness, optimism, with a *little* ability, to get through this world?

"The trouble with the whole Kinnan and Traphagen outfit is that we are too modest and sensitive. We are too conscious of our limitations, instead of forgetting that we have any. Your father always under-estimated himself and his possibilities, too conscious of his shortcomings."

The girl smiled ruefully to herself. That was her mother's polite way, now he was dead, of lamenting his social and financial failure. She wrote:

"Dear Mother:

I think you would concede me my meed of gall, aggressiveness and optimism, if you could see me throwing my writings at distinguished editors, assuring them that if they would read them, they would certainly give me a job.

"Honore Willsie Morrow is a great Juno-esque woman like Aunt Madeline, with blue-black hair parted in the middle. She read Dodge's letter and smiled—I wish I'd peeked at it—and then read one or two of my things. She said, 'Well, you've got the gift of gab all right. Only God Almighty can tell you whether you'll do anything with it or not. I suppose you are too young to know that you have to have something to say. You have to have some private gospel that you want terribly to preach. I don't mean moralizing. I mean that there has to be something close to your heart that you want to talk about. Now mine is Nature. In all my fiction, I'm filled with the desire to make other people see nature as beautifully as I know I see it!'

"She advised me to get any kind of job in the world except a literary job. She said, 'Go ahead and live and work, and if you've got the spark in you, it'll burn you up until you let it out. You'll be wild to get at your writing. You'll sit up nights to do it. If you do hack stuff in a magazine office, you'll go stale.'

"She didn't know of any job for me. I'm trying *Harper's* and the *Century* to-morrow."

Ida wrote:

"I can't help but feel that Mrs. Morrow gave you very poor advice. Surely it will mean literary advancement for you if you are in contact with editors and other writers. They tell me contact is *most* important in selling stories."

From Marjorie:

"Philip Littell on the *New Republic* turned me over helplessly to Francis Hackett and his new blonde Scandinavian wife, Signe Toksvig. They spent an hour calling up people who would be willing to give me audience. They have just been married but she is going right on with her work. It was funny to see them. She is perfectly beautiful and he's big and sort of shaggily bearlike with poppy eyes, as if he ought to be a scientist. He leaned over her as if he could eat her up, but he called her Miss Toksvig and was frightfully formal. She called him Mr. Hackett and didn't dare look at him, and acted like a prim little school teacher. They sent me Monday to James Oppenheim. He said what Mrs. Morrow did, in a different way. He said, 'You have the writer's gift. I can't tell you any more than that.'

"He advised me to go in for psycho-analysis. Said it was the greatest thing in the world for a writer, to help him probe into human motives and emotions. He sent me right over to a woman psycho-analyst on Gramercy Park, Dr.——. She has a gorgeous office, full of cabinets of records and with a couch where people lie while she hypnotizes them. She needs a literary secretary, to answer her mail and, in time, to write a book, phrase it, that is, from her notes. At first I thought it was a priceless opportunity. But her nails were bitten to the quick, and her hands trembled, and she pointed to her cabinets and whispered, 'If you work for me you've got to know AWFUL things about people,' and it gave me the creeps. I told her I didn't think the job would be good for me, and she flew into a rage. So that was that. You ought to be pleased. Lord knows it wouldn't be the kind of writing you like—sweet and simple.

"Yesterday the Hackett's sent me to Eugene Saxton, editor of the *Bookman*. He was noncommittal and I felt quite encouraged. Said he would let me know. I'm getting a little anxious and I guess I showed it. I felt as I went out that I had acted young and oh, undesirable. Sure enough, a polite little note from him this morning. 'Sorry, no vacancy.' You see, if I were good enough, these people would *make* a vacancy. Never mind, I'm not discouraged."

Later.

"My dear Mother:

I hate to confess what a silly thing has happened to me. I stopped in a shop way up Broadway to try on a hat that I saw in the window. I laid down my purse and my portfolio—the hat was darling—and when I turned around my purse was gone. Just like any other country girl in the big city. I'm so ashamed. And it was such an insult for them to take the money and leave the manuscripts, as if they knew which had the highest value!

"'Who steals my purse, steals trash, but he who robs me of my good name—that's tommyrot. I would feel all puffed up if it had been the manuscripts to go!

"Yes, my last nickel was in it. I had just spent forty dollars of it for a military wrist watch for Chuck, and the watch was in the purse, and all my other money. And my 'rejection slip' from Mr. Saxton that I wrote you about. I hope the thief got home and felt badly to think it was a poor girl looking for a job.

"I had hurried off without breakfast and it was after twelve o'clock. The only person I dared bother was Miss Toksvig. I walked all the way from up town down to the *New Republic,* and when I told her about it I was so tired and hungry I burst out crying. Lord, what a fool! She kissed me and insisted on loaning me a ten dollar bill. I asked her how she could be sure I'd ever repay it. She laughed and said, never mind if I didn't. She said, 'Some day you may have a chance to do the same thing for some other young soul just starting out and in trouble. Then you will think of this, and that will be the payment.' Of course, I'll get it back to her the very first thing I do.

"The joke of it was, I went out with my ten dollar bill and had a cup of chocolate and a sandwich at the first little shop, and they couldn't change the bill, and told me to go on, they would stand treat. And on the trolley car going home the conductor couldn't change it either, and I rode free!

"Don't worry about me. I wired Chuck and he wired me back his two months' pay, all he had."

The letter was torture to Ida. A fight for life like this had ceased to be amusing. What had she gotten the girl into? And damn Chuck, anyway! She wrote:

"My dear Daughter:

I am astonished and hurt that you should turn to anyone but me in such an emergency as the one you have just described. Surely it would have been in better taste to have notified me, rather than a young man in a training camp. What would people say?

"You do need a new hat. I was not satisfied with what you had when I left you. I'm enclosing a check, and if 'Chuck', as he is so crudely called, is supplying you with living funds, you had better use this for a new hat, et cetera. Keep up your appearance. You will find a readier admission everywhere if you are well-dressed and *sparkling*. It may be necessary to remind you that regardless of the help behind you of your Camp Upton private's salary, your mother will always be glad to see that you do not go hungry."

Ida was chagrined that after all, it was Imogene, one of the "sisters", who got her daughter her job. Marjorie wrote that she ran into Imogene on Fifth Avenue. Imogene had a good job on the War Work Council of the National Y.W.C.A. doing magazine publicity and she said:

"You're looking for a job? Ye gods, come on over to the Y. and I'll get you one writing magazine articles. They give you the material, letters and facts from overseas and we write them up and sneak in a mention of the Y.W. as often but as quietly as we can, and the publicity director places them with the magazines. It's a cinch."

Elizabeth Wyckoff glanced at Marjorie's material, stories, and essays, largely from the "Lit", carried around New York until they wore beggar's tatters.

"That's all right," she said laconically. "As long as you can use the King's English. We're not fussy. Imo, when I send her back from Paddy's office, put the new slave to work."

"Paddy" was the fierce dragon who clung, in the hysteria of the war, to the "old" standards of the organization. She had been head of the publicity bureau during the years when its advertising consisted of pictures of girls in gym bloomers, on the camp page of the Sunday papers.

"Paddy has to look in your face and make sure you're a Christian, before I hire you," drawled Mrs. Wyckoff.

On the threshold of the sacred office, she whispered to the girl, "If you're not a member of a Protestant Evangelical Church, you'd better be, if you want to draw a salary from this bunch. Rule of the gang."

"What's a Protestant Evangelical Church?"

"Baptists, Methodists, and Presbyterians. Unitarian won't do."

"All right. Let's see. I'm a Baptist."

"Good girl."

It was not what Ida would have wished. But it had dignity, she could tell of it without shame, and shortly the girl's name began appearing in the women's magazines over such titles as "The Little Grey Hut with the Blue Triangle" and "With the Y.W.C.A. Through Three Revolutions in Russia."

Never mind the sloppy sentimentality, the cheap journalistic style. Never mind that when the girl needed extra money she dashed off an off-color story for "Snappy Stories". Her stuff was "selling" and she was "in print".

In April 1919 Ida received a letter whose very envelope had an ominous look. She handed it to Arthur.

"Open it, son. I have the feeling it's bad news."

"My dear Mother:

Just a note to let you know that Chuck and I are going to be married a week from Thursday. His job with the Federal Export Company promises to be permanent, so we decided we might as well do it now. You might as well know that he only has $25 a week, but with my $25 that makes $50 and surely two people can live very comfortably on that. We have taken a charming apartment just east of Fifth Avenue, nice enough even for you not to be snippy about it. We sub-leased it, way below cost", etc. etc.

Ida's mouth went dry as it had the night of Arthur's death. Then with her last ounce of courage, vitriol of her pen. She was almost done.

"Oh my daughter—

If you do this thing, this mad thing, this wasting of yourself on that sullen stripling, never reproach me with not having warned you of the consequences. If you do it, you are doomed.

"I awoke last night in a cold sweat. I had dreamt that I saw you falling down a steep flight of stairs, down and down. I could not stop you, I could not save you, I could only watch that fatal plunge. When I reached you at the foot you were white and limp—I can see it now—with your slim neck broken. This morning—your letter. I am not a superstitious woman, but surely the omen must frighten you, as it does me.

"Get out of this folly and I will do anything for you that you may ask—spend part of my principal to take you abroad—anything."

She could not see the girl and the sullen stripling laughing themselves into each other's arms over the flight of stairs and the slim broken neck.

"Dear Mother:

Sorry. Thursday."

Ida put Arthur out to board, like the family dog or cat, and took the next train to New York. She was defeated. The battle was over. She had thought that if this child to whose success she had dedicated herself, hoisted at last, in spite of everything she could do, the enemy's flag, she would not care whether she ever laid eyes on her again. She had created this girl's body as few are created. She had fondly hoped that she was creating her mind. She had toiled with her, a stubborn clay, to make her into the image of her dreams. Now it was all over. There was an alien soul there with which she had no concern. This strange female creature was blood of her blood, bone of her bone, flesh of her flesh—but the spirit around which blood, bone, and flesh were built, was a fragment broken off from the cosmic consciousness and was not hers at all.

She had been an insolent woman, daring the universe for her petty desires. Now she was broken. She was the human mother of a human child. She only knew that her bowels yearned over her, that she must not lose her altogether, and that like any other woman, she must be on hand for her she-child's giving away in marriage. She loved her daughter; with or without glory, she loved her.

She reached New York in time to console herself with the buying of an outfit for the girl. She and the enemy kept an armed truce until the ceremony should be over. The enemy was courteous and distant and so was she. The night before, she sat with the girl in her room and tried to draw her out on the subject of the prevention of the added calamity of children. Surely she hoped not to add children to the difficulties she would find herself faced with.

No. The girl was cold and remote. No. She would acknowledge their undesirability at this time. She was fully prepared. She had reliable sources of information.

Was she certain? Ida herself could help her very little. Her father— she faltered into details—wonderful self-control.

The girl stamped her foot.

"I never heard of anything so horrible! Don't come here spoiling my happiness with your disgusting stories of your married life!"

Ida was maddened by the girl's assumption of superiority. She narrowed her eyes. She suspected from the surface indifference of this man and girl, the existence of the shocking element of passion.

"Oh don't pretend," she sneered, "to be so awfully pure."

The girl's nerve, worn ragged by the ever-present conflict, snapped to pieces. To her horror, she saw herself, like her very ghost, stride over to the woman and say "Damn you!" and slap her face.

In a moment she recovered herself and was sick with compunction. She gathered the woman's bony frame into her arms and smothered her face with kisses. Why couldn't she have kept her hate in leash? Oh, the poor soul—.

Ida sat with tears streaming down her face, unmoving, a hound that has been struck and will let you, if you wish, strike him again.

"Mother, you shouldn't have tormented me to-night. I'm so tired—I didn't know what I was doing. It wasn't I—just think that it wasn't I— you know I didn't mean it. Forgive me!"

Yes, she would forgive her. She would forgive her anything.

The ceremony, out of the driving rain, before a driveling assistant pastor, was a nightmare to the three of them. The little pastor congratulated her on her acquisition of this fine son to take over the sacred care of her daughter. There was a torturing wedding supper Ida had sent in from Sherry's. The delicate food might have been straw in their mouths. Ida left alone that night, to go home and go on with Arthur. She was wearing the orchids the enemy had sent her. She thanked him with attempted graciousness, but the dynamite sizzled beneath.

"Your first orchids?" he answered. "Don't tell me, Mrs. Kinnan," he went on grimly, "with your insistence on putting on style, that no one has ever sent you orchids before."

"That was no reason," she answered wearily, "why I didn't want them for her."

He was touched.

"Don't take it so to heart. I'll never give her wealth, or position. But some day in my own way—not yours—there may be success. But we're going to have a Hell of a good time."

She shook her head through her tears. They simply didn't speak the same language.

Interlude

Ida was reconciled, from now on, to her daughter's inability to report any startling success for herself or her husband. He had another job now——. She had another job now——. They had saved a few hundred dollars and were seriously considering spending the winter in a cabin in the mountains of North Carolina, to see what they could do at joint authorship. Chuck called it wryly, "turning our backs on commerce and industry." Marjorie had a publicity job with Doran, the publishing house. No, she wasn't writing much, just odds and ends. Her stuff had something so definitely the matter with it. She couldn't seem to tell what. Marjorie would have to leave the Doran job. They had decided to accept an offer to Chuck to go to Louisville as advertising manager of a large department store. It paid well, and their feet were rather itching. It had been Louisville or the Carolina mountains, and they had agreed to give commerce and industry another try.

Ida could not resist a sly attack on the enemy.

"My dear Daughter:

"Well, M— has made her visit here and I enjoyed it very much. If one half that she tells me is true, which I believe, her husband is certainly arriving. He is Manager of the Chicago and Minneapolis offices for the Bankers Trust of New York. One week of every month he spends in Minneapolis. To-morrow he joins M— here for Homecoming and is to address the mass meeting to-morrow night in the Gym, which of course pleases his little wife.

"Marjorie, their relationship seems *ideal*.

"She admits frankly that she is not in love nor ever pretended to be and he knows it. He also has had several affairs, 'a most engrossing one in France', so he was in the same position as she. But they seem to be harmoniously congenial and she is *very* proud of him. But she said 'Oh, ye gods, Mother Kinnan, he's homely; so homely that it makes your face ache to look at him.' She was here from Monday until Wednesday and had two letters from P— in Minneapolis. He calls her 'Babe'.

"After they return to Chicago next week they are going into a furnished apartment, five rooms and sun parlor, $150 a month. She has engaged a maid, $10 a week. They have arranged to put P—'s grandmother aged 82 into a private sanitarium and M— said that would cost them about $150 a month. You can figure for yourself what his salary must hover around. He will have to go to New York once every two months and M— will go with him when she needs clothes, as she wants to keep in touch with her wonderful modiste who has been making her clothes.

"Now don't get sick just yet, for that is only about P—.

"For diversion, M— has taken up short story writing. She brought her first effort, all typewritten, ready for the *Saturday Evening Post,* for me to read as she 'values opinion and criticism.' She is sending it first to the *Post* because she thinks it is a *Post* story and through the intimate acquaintance and friendship of George Patullo, a regular contributor to the *Post*, she expects to have it accepted. Through P—'s football experience, his most remarkable war record and his business success, they seem really to know a great many worth-while, well-known personages. Did you know that P— was news courier for the Peace Conference in Paris? George Patullo's wife and Coach Richard's wife are sisters and M— said they always saw much of them all when they were in New York. The two women recently inherited from their father's estate, two million apiece.

"Well, to return to the story. I have read *in print* much worse ones. Wouldn't it be funny, actually weird, if she should actually *sell* it? Oh my dear!!!

"She and P— were members of the 'Beechwood Players' through Mr. Keys with whom he went to Europe. In one of their plays, M— had the lead. When she came out in the last act, dressed in a gorgeous white satin dinner gown, 'there was an audible gasp' from the audience. 'Of course, it was the gown.'

"She has calmed down a great deal. She is settled in life. She thinks that she is happier than she would have been, had she married R— with whom she was 'most romantically in love'. She is proud of P— because he makes worthwhile friends and she is sure now he is going to be a financial success and provide her with luxuries. And he doesn't get on her nerves. R— certainly gave her the jolt of her life, and she is only recovering. She isn't as fit physically as she used to be, and the sparkle in her eyes is gone. She has a funny little face and last summer she bobbed her hair. She is doing it up now by pinning on a switch and wearing a net. It seems thin and lies flat to her head. You remember, her hair was always rather pretty?

"Well, well! How the wheel of fortune does turn and one never knows in front of whom it is going to stop.

"A few weeks ago, in Chicago, P— went into a financial concern to see the manager whose name is Harris. The lady clerk in the outer office told P— when he handed her his card to take into her chief that she didn't think he could possibly see Mr. Harris that day as he was very busy. Just then the door of Mr. Harris' private sanctum opened and out stepped Carl Harris. He is making about fifteen thousand a year! P— had no idea that the august Mr. Harris whose patronage he was soliciting was the poor little Carl Harris the Beta's wouldn't pledge. It's an interesting old world after all, isn't it?"

And in a later letter:

"M— and P— were here for dinner—

"Now here is a surprise. I like P—. He seems very much the gentleman, very much at ease, without any ostentation, a good conversationalist and perfectly groomed. His contact with the world and personages of note have left their impress. He is self assured without any show of egotism—and he seems genuinely fond of his wife without any effort at 'effect'. He addresses her always in a perfectly natural manner as 'dear', considers her comfort and wishes, insofar as they do not interfere with the important business which he has on hand."

She soon discovered that her daughter punished her for what she thought she had done so subtly, by not answering these letters. That was slow torture. To go out to the mail box in the hall, after she had heard the postman click the cover, trying to get there ahead of the "two nice girls" who still made the apartment possible—and find no thick letter with the beloved scrawl.

She would write:

"My dear daughter:

"It has been six weeks since I heard from you. If you think that our viewpoints on life are so far apart that you want to break with me permanently, please let me know. This not writing me at all is cruel—and you know it."

Then the reward would come.

"Dear foolish mother:

"If you can get your mind off gorgeous white satin dinner dresses long enough to talk reasonably our correspondence can fly thick and fast."

But old habit was strong and in February of 1921 the girl made her first visit home to her mother since her marriage—for the sole secret reason that she had a new gray squirrel coat. Ida was so happy that she could only hover around her and offer her breakfast in bed. The girl showed a bright surfaced affection for her but she seemed strange and talked more wildly than ever before.

"You know, Mother, I'm not a genius, but I think it quite possible that I might be the mother of a genius."

Ida was horrified. "I hope nothing—"

"No, I'm speaking from the abstract viewpoint."

"But aren't you begging the issue? Wouldn't that be doing what you've accused me of doing in you. Making another person try to live the life you failed to live?"

"No. Genius can't be forced. I only mean that there is something vital in me that must find ultimate expression. If not in me, then later. Perhaps it began with you. You know, Mother, I stopped writing for a while. I'm not ready to write. I'm full of theories about people that I've got to prove or disprove by living and studying a little longer. I want to write books about things I don't know enough about yet.

"Perhaps I'll only live my books. Life seems to me an exploration, an expedition into the unknown. One's enjoyment and profit of it depend on one's like or dislike of mental travel."

Ida smiled tolerantly and shook her head.

The girl visited some of her old classes and professors. She said to Dodge:

"I've stopped being in such an awful hurry to write and 'get on the market'. There isn't the rush I thought there was. You know I think a great deal of the present successful writing by young authors is only the exuberance of youth. They simply bubble over into print."

He laughed. "Of course in such cases, their writing wouldn't be what we call 'the real thing'. It wouldn't last."

He twinkled professional heresy at her. "Does it matter anyway?"

The girl's visit ended abruptly. The enemy, in Louisville, became uneasy. His wife was being exposed again to the smallpox. And anyhow, he couldn't have her away so long—he wanted her back——. There was a long distance call and the daughter packed and left with an unseemly eagerness.

⚒

Arthur's graduation. The little Buick.

"I haven't had many rides, but Arthur feels very important running around."

Sacrifice had become as much of a habit as air and water. The trip East with the boy, "stopping at the best hotels after so many years of feeling poor."

Ida left her son in the East to make his way as her daughter four years before had made hers, and turned back alone to the scene of her battles. She might have stayed in New York and "made a home" for the boy. But he too was emotionally involved and she feared such enforced supervision would only hasten his marriage. Let him be a man among men, free of women's apron strings. She was strong enough to say goodbye to him, her only comfort, and go back to Madison.

Loneliness and Knowledge

"I did not know it would be so empty. I was not prepared."

Ida was taken unawares by the Madison apartment she had come back to close. Four years before there had been the suffering of seeing her daughter pass beyond the horizon like an outbound ship. There had been just now her lesser reluctance to part with the boy she had so newly found. When she opened the door on the musty smell of the college home, in September of 1922, it was like opening the door of a tomb.

Marjorie might have lain there, laid out in the pussywillow taffeta with the gold embroidery and the golden slippers. Arthur might have lain dead there; Arthur with his shy touch on her arm and the quick nervous ways of his father; the boy Arthur.

People had said, "Won't you mind going back to Madison alone?" And with her thought on her children's welfare, she had said simply, "It seems the thing to do. Marjorie has no place for me in her life, and I want the boy to get a start alone."

She planned to sell everything but a chair or two, perhaps a table, the clock and candlesticks, and the odds and ends of linens and silver that had survived her more pretentious days. She thought it desirable to keep enough to furnish a single room, wherever she might be. She had it in her mind to go back to Fenton some day, when her mother and father had outlived their independence and their quarrelsomeness, and take care of them, among the last few friends of her childhood.

Ed and Fanny were there, and Mag. Sister Flo was dead, but Mabel was near, and Ethel, and dear old Clarence and funny old Liew, doctors both. She felt closer to them than at any time since her girlhood.

It would be cozy to go back home again. She had been so glad to get away and she would be so glad to go back. Pa and Ma had sold the farm, but their little house in Fenton smelled of cookies and honey and stone jars of fried cakes just the same. The crocks of butter sat on the cellar floor, the pickles and preserves swung on a shelf over them.

Pa sat reading or brooding most of the time, except when he was splitting wood for three years ahead, or fussing in his perfect garden. Ma was as pretty and as infuriating as ever.

But they did not need her yet. Meantime, she had thought with something like relief that her work was done. She could give some thought to herself. She could have pretty clothes. She would make friends. She could lie in bed in the morning and then go out to breakfast to the Chocolate Shop. She could have manicures, and her hair waved. She could eat a box of candy all alone, without a trace of guilt. There would be theatres and concerts and a little travel.

She would stay in Madison for a while. Marjorie's sorority had asked her to live at the house as chaperon this coming year. She had accepted as a mere time-filler. Besides, it would leave all her income free for luxuries. For luxuries for herself. She would be able to send the children gorgeous boxes at Christmas.

Yes, she would spend this year in Madison. She was reluctant to leave the familiar ground—just yet.

And now the familiar ground was revealed for itself—a battleground, with the ghosts of her dead to haunt her.

All that first night she paced up and down in the desolate apartment, and wrung her hands and fought for breath.

Certainly, life had not prepared her for anything like this.

She wrote her daughter from the sorority house, after her first few weeks:

"The girls are wonderful to me. Everything possible is done for my happiness and comfort. I have three new gowns, really very handsome. You would not know me. There was a big rushing dinner last night. The day before, the girls insisted that I decide which evening dress I would wear. I chose the showiest, they seemed so anxious, the one of black tulle and sequins. It turned out they wanted to be sure to send me harmonious flowers. My bouquet was violets, with an orchid in the center. The *second* time in my life I have ever had an orchid.

"I have all the time I want, for the first time in my life. Nothing to do but dress well and be a lady. I thought I would love it. But oh my dear, all I want is my home and children back again! None of it is any fun. When I sit in Mrs. Harley's beauty shop getting my hair done, I wish it was you, and that I was in the apartment waiting for you. I would take back all the hard work and heartache, if it were possible."

For the first time, a pitying love swept across the daughter. She could picture only too well the stiff and lonely woman in the midst of chattering youth. What were parties to her now, parties for other women's daughters; their dates; their engagements; their murmurings? Marjorie had dismissed her mother from her mind as "nicely taken care of". Now she understood that the woman was more forlorn in this light-hearted house of youth than in the center of the sea. She had lived too long in other lives, and the penalty now was loneliness.

She could not know that her daughter was seized with a sudden panic; that she felt she could not let this pitiful woman who had borne her, go on any longer, so alone; that a bell far back in the core of her spirit tinkled a warning that if she waited, she would be too late—. Ida only knew that when she thought she could not endure life any longer, letters began to come regularly from the daughter to whom correspondence hitherto had been only a desultory duty. Letters twice a week. A special delivery on Sunday mornings, timed exactly.

One Sunday morning there was a box of roses. She held it half opened, after one look at the scrawled message within. She could only sit woodenly, holding on to herself, nodding and grimacing, and answering to questions only, lest she choke and betray herself,

"My daughter—"

She did not remember that her last letter had begun:

"I have just come up to my room. These are the lonely moments, unless I have something *special* to do. One can not *read* and *rest* all the time.

"This has been 'Homecoming' you know, and the crowds and enthusiasm increase as the years go by. There were so many people back whom I knew when you were here. You know I knew very few people well. I stayed so closely at home. But they all acted as if they knew me quite well."

Her daughter did not intend to shame her with her neglect before all these people who acted as if they knew her quite well. But she must hurry, she must hurry.

> "823 Irving Court
> Madison Wis.
> 4 P.M. Thanksgiving Day

"My dear dear daughter:

"Bless your heart! for the Thanksgiving message. The wire was handed me just after breakfast. How thoughtful and *dear* you are! If I could have had just a word from Arthur, the day would have gone very well—

"Do you know this is the first Thanksgiving that I have ever spent away from him? (22 years)

"We had a wonderful dinner here, really as nice as any dinner could be. The girls asked me if I would carve the turkey so that it could be brought to the table whole. Some of the girls had flowers, gorgeous chrysanthemums and roses, huge bouquets; so that the house looked very festive and then I poured the coffee in the parlor after dinner. It was all very lovely.

"And I have gotten through the day very well, just haven't had time to think of past Thanksgivings—

"And your lovely message was such a help and such a surprise—"

Past Thanksgivings! The girl, too, was filled with nostalgia for them. Crisp Washington days, with the red leaves often still on the trees; the earth firm and good under your feet; the chestnuts on the ground. Aunt Jenny and Uncle Will always came, with Aunt Jenny's father, Mr. Fish, with a bottle of beer tucked under his coat for Ida, and his joke about it. Aunt Jenny's sealskin jacket, and how soft and cool it was to bury your nose in it. Uncle Will taking Father's hand and saying with his little chuckle, "Well, Arthur—", and loving him with his look.

Ida always washed her curtains for Thanksgiving. Sometimes they were only put up on the morning itself, crisp and starched like little girls' petticoats. The great roast turkey from the farm. The "fixin's". The sweet cold cider. Ida's hustle and bustle and her clean dress and her trying to keep her hair in curl, over the steam. And after the dinner, Ida's annual refusal to touch the dishes until the next day. Mr. Fish nodding in the corner. Ida and Jenny going aside into the bedroom and talking fascinating woman things in low voices. Father and Uncle Will content and intimate. Mr. Fish dropping to sleep at last, and little Arthur being sick—

And Christmas almost the same, except that it was at Aunt Jenny's house, and they sat afterward in the upstairs sitting room by the grate fire.

The letter went on:

"Now listen, if you really *want* to come to see me, I'll pay your fare one way and let it come as part of your Christmas present. And you may take advantage of the offer whenever you like, with *one* stipulation. If you are contented and having a good time, you are not to be ordered home long distance, just as you nicely get here. I won't waste my money that way.

"If you do not find a dress that you like, wait until you get here and we will shop together. Now that you have nothing to do, I should think you could come any time.

"I have wondered often today how you might be spending Thanksgiving and if you were happy—

"I have been interrupted—

"Girls came in to talk and your cousin Bob called up and wanted me to go out to supper and to a movie with him, and so the evening went. I thought perhaps he might be lonesome or maybe your Aunt Luella told him to ask me, thinking I'd be forlorn. She's so thoughtful and such a diplomat too.

"I have a beautiful, fragrant pink rosebud facing me on my table, in the silver bud vase you gave me for Christmas, years ago, and nearly took my breath away by paying five dollars for it when we were hard up—

"One of the girls brought it in to me from her bouquet. The rose, I mean.

"Only three weeks now, to Christmas vacation. The time is going rapidly.

"You hardly know how I appreciate your thoughtfulness.

"Love from Mother."

"823 Irving Court
Madison Wis.
Dec. 4, 1922

"My dear daughter:

"Aren't we getting chummy in our declining years?

"I'm afraid of the reaction, or a time when we'll get so busy again or something that we'll fall back into the old way of not writing often to each other.

"There I go again, at my old habit of joy-killing.

"Well, I don't exactly mean it; just one of my little jokes, you know— my kind—

"You were a *dear* to send the Special. It always helps a lot. I think I've read it six times to be sure I got every word and interpreted it all right.

"Yesterday I received a letter from Aunt Mabel Stecker inviting me to spend Christmas with them. I mean, all of my vacation. She also has asked Aunt Marjorie in Muskegon and intends to ask Bob. He will not go tho'. He gets bored and can't smoke.

"Lovingly, Mother."

But she decided, after all, to go "home" for Christmas. She knew that Grandma would drive her crazy, but she wanted to see her.

She was taking long walks now, in the winter twilight. She wasn't feeling right, she had been X-rayed and blood-tested, to no purpose. She needed to put on weight. She found she could slip away from the sorority house in the late afternoon, before dinner, and walk out to the Ag. buildings with a little enamel pail and get fresh rich milk to drink.

She had never walked alone before. Odd, how strange this country was to her, after all these years. Of course, she hadn't gotten out much, before.

She hadn't known how beautiful that hill was, topped with pine trees, with a star or the early glowing sunset through them, or the new moon; the hill dipping down on one side to a gentle valley, on the other to the lake, smooth and crystal with ice and snow.

Ah, Ida, life is fooling you! Beauty has slipped up on you unawares. It is impossible to walk alone at twilight over snowy hills and not find Beauty.

There is a new note in her letters. They are sad and lonely, but they are quiet. The fever and fret have gone.

"I did not know that so little could matter to me, that mattered before."

She has learned that the schemes of man are fatuous and impudent, and unacceptable to the nostrils of the gods.

Old battlefields are always peaceful.

She has lost her fight, but here are love, and peace of soul, and beauty. She only asks now the loving letters, and the promise of the visit, and the walks at twilight over the Wisconsin hills.

Somehow the telegram from Fenton, Michigan, is not a surprise to the daughter.

"Mother's condition serious. Come. Uncle Clarence."

There have been warnings of this. The haste, oh the haste to be kind! Somehow, months ago, the rustling of wings—

Ida opens half-seeing eyes from her agony, from her merciful impending unconsciousness. She points in triumph, nodding with satisfaction to those around her.

"My daughter! My daughter—"

She struggles to the last, since struggle has become so much a habit. Fight, even when you can't see why—

Abram goes out into the woodshed and beats his gaunt bony fists on the cordwood he has split.

Fanny wails up and down like an old peasant hag.

"Oh Idy! She came home to her mother's arms to die! Her mother closed her eyes!"

She shrieks, half-hoping that much of Fenton will hear.

"Oh Idy! She was so intelligent!"

The little blonde English nurse draws Dr. Clarence aside in her distress. She hadn't wanted an infectious throat case, anyway. She was just getting over tonsillitis herself. And now this was her third death in a row. Really, doctor, a nurse minds deaths dreadfully.

And Arthur is a little late. Just in time to put his hand on her arm with his shy boy's touch.

"It's a rotten deal," he says to his sister. "She was just beginning to learn things."

Never mind, if she was learning.

Beauty, and peace of soul, and love.

There have been generals who have not fought so desperately; heroes without half the courage; famous folk who have lived splendidly, and have not learned so much.